The Devil's Nose

Luz Argentina Chiriboga

Translated by
Ingrid Watson Miller and Margaret L. Morris

PAGE PUBLISHING, INC.
New York, NY

Originally published by Page Publishing, Inc. 2015

ISBN 978-1-63417-690-3 (pbk)
ISBN 978-1-63417-691-0 (digital)

Printed in the United States of America

In Memory of
Dempsey and Matilda Watson
And
George and Lillie Mae Lindsay

ACKNOWLEDGEMENTS

This project could not have been completed without the support of several people. We would first like to thank Luz Argentina Chiriboga, Ecuador's first Afro-Ecuadorian woman novelist, for permission to translate her work *La nariz del diablo*. We appreciate her support and confidence in us to bring her novel to an American audience.

We appreciate the technical and editing support and the language assistance of Dr. Josefina González.

Last, but not least, we thank our husbands, George Miller and Richard Morris, who are always encouraging us to soar to new heights in our field

CHAPTER ONE

Kingston, September 8, 1900, *Saint Mary Day.*[1]

*T*he news spreads rapidly in Jamaica. Representatives of the Guayaquil and Quito Railway Company are calling for laborers to go to work in Ecuador, a country located in South America. Contractors MacDonald and H. Killan have gone to the harbor to offer such an important job opportunity to build the railway line.[2] They promise good wages, proper treatment, and safety.

---

[1]   The actual construction of the railroad began in the late 1890s, but the indigenous workers refused to leave their homes and families. Representatives of the American company, The Guayaquil and Quito Railroad Co., went to Jamaica to convince the Jamaicans of a great job opportunity.

St Mary is one of the smallest parishes on the northeastern coast of Jamaica.

"Quito-Guayaquil Railroad." In Thomas M. Leonard, ed. *Encyclopedia of Latin America: Search for National Identity*, vol. 3. New York: Facts On File, Inc., 2010. *Modern World History Online.* Facts On File, Inc. http://www.fofweb.com/activelink2.asp?ItemID=WE53&iPin=ELAIII0318&SingleRecord=True (accessed December 2, 2012).

[2]   James MacDonald initially tried to hire Chinese to build the railroad, but the Ecuadorian government was opposed to so many Chinese entering the country. MacDonald then went to Jamaica in 1900, because he believed that "the blacks were considered to be better suited to heavy construction work than the local Indians due to the nature of the work and the tropical climate." A. Kim Clark. *The Redemptive Work: Railway and Nation in Ecuador, 1895–1930* (Wilmington, Del.: Scholarly Resources, Inc., 1998), 90.

Men approach in order to find out what it is all about; nobody knows where Ecuador is. For the Marret brothers, Gregory and Syne, their mind is running while they consider what the contractors tell them and they begin to understand the proposal.

The timbre of Mr. MacDonald's voice sounds enticing, and the offer is of prime importance—the work place is safe, and the pay is on time. "Ecuador is a beautiful, beautiful country. And there is a lot of gold!" says the contractor, and the group of laborers does not miss a word. He talks about the musicality of the songs of birds, of the song of the rivers, of the towering Andes, of the simple and humble people who live there. Mr. MacDonald says they will be given housing, food, and good treatment.

"Is there any danger? Are there abysses?" asks Syne.

"No, there is gold and good treatment," insists the contractor.

The enthusiasm that they unveil in order to conquer the laborers is notorious: they fuel the imagination of all Jamaicans to ensnare them.

"Four *reales* daily. A fortune, a fortune," adds Killan.

The laborers are fascinated with the proposal. Excited, they discuss the idea of going to earn money; and it costs them to conceal their joy since it constitutes an opportunity to improve their economic situation, and they know that there is no other way to escape from poverty. The laborers nod their head and smile; it must have seemed like a miracle to the *gringos* since they need five thousand laborers for the construction of the railway line.[3]

The contractors' proposal is impressive—which, without other explanation or contradiction, convinces the Jamaicans. MacDonald and Killan test their skill, their own art of good negotiating. They are always calm, always smiling, and always tolerant—qualities that are essential to achieve success. No more explanation is needed; there is an explicit covenant—not to mention or to offer more, the main objective

---

[3]   It is believed that approximately 4,000 men from Jamaica, as well as a few of the other island nations, traveled to Ecuador to take the railway up the 12,000 foot peak known as "The Devil's Nose." Galo García Idrovo, "El Ferrocarril más difícil del mundo: la ruta en la cuenca del río Chanchán," en: Sonia Fernández Rueda, compiladora, *El Ferrocarril de Alfaro. El sueño de integración*, (Quito, Tehis-Corporación Editora Nacional, 2008), 142.

is the main objective. They have succeeded in convincing the laborers to get involved in the construction of the railway in Ecuador.

However, Gregory Marret holds off on commenting on the adventure because that would be a situation totally different from what he is living. Reflective, he walks toward his home—where he hopes his wife, Pamela, and his children, David and Edna, are waiting for him. He wonders whether it will be ridiculous to leave his family and his country to go after this tale of traveling to Ecuador. Stunned and with a feeling of nostalgia, he doubts the desirability of the matter. Nevertheless, he points out the need to raise money to buy a plot of land and set up a house for his family.

Upon reaching the hut where he lives, he drops down at the entrance from where he sees the sunlight fading. Pamela's loving lips stamp their mark on her husband's cheek, and she looks at him so thoughtfully as if his open spirit were leaving, floating. Concerned, she asks what happened; and after a long time, he tells her of the project to travel to a distant country located in South America. They do nothing but discuss the benefits that the money would bring them. He hopes to save money, buy land, build a home, and work a small farm where he would sow corn, coffee, *cacao*. The idea is enchanting, for their dreams would come true. Gregory understands that without that salary, he would never acquire property.

The next day, Gregory feels dizzy, empty, and cowardly. Should he go to the contractors' offices to register? Should he go, or should he not? Breathing heavily, he looks at the skyline stunned. He has the impression that his body is floating in the void in order to then fall. He walks into the office and finds a very long line of people who want to travel to Ecuador.

So he decides it is better to look for work at the harbor. He moves on thoughtfully with his head hung between his shoulders. Arriving there, he supports his body on a wall, waiting to be called for any job; however, he waits in vain that day because there is no opportunity for work. Fear begins to beat him; he thinks of hunger, of diseases, and he goes back to entertaining the idea of traveling to Ecuador. It is as if he were down at the bottom of a hidden lake, and he was listening to his own silence and the voice of the Andes.

He should go to sign up as soon as possible, or they will leave without him; but until then, he isn't very convinced to take the journey. Sometimes he wants to be rejected by the contractors. He is frightened, and he suspects that they have not told him the whole truth. *Why come so far to look for black men?* It is impossible to know what kinds of jobs they are really going to perform. It is something that he should ask. Two days later, he returns to the harbor. This time, he is lucky because they hire him for three days of work; the previous evening cargo ships had arrived loaded with merchandise. He realizes that it is always better to work near his family and see his children grow up.

He trembles at the thought that his brother and his friends are accepting the offer of work, and he is staying. A man throws him a bundle, and he quickly takes it to the storeroom in the rear. He comes and goes with cargo until nightfall. He smiles satisfied because of the money he earned. As he leaves the harbor, he finds his brother Syne, who wonders why he hasn't even registered for the trip abroad, and informs him that he is ready to go.

Gregory thinks about it and ensures him that he will be going to sign up soon. He says goodbye and hurries off. From that moment, he will never doubt the benefits that going so far away to work will bring his family. His brother thinks of nothing but that project and counts the hours left until he realizes that dream. If he could sail that night, he would be happy because he has no wife or children.

It's almost the end of the afternoon, and the contractors' office is closing. Gregory moves along the waterfront to find a long line of men ready to embark. Some are carrying bundles of clothes, others small cartons; and many are leaving with packages wrapped in only banana leaves. Jamaican laborers come from all parts of the country. Scared, they look anxiously; their eyes, black and bright as the noonday light, show nervousness; their usual smile has disappeared from their lips. For a long time, Gregory watches them. He feels hesitant; an external force stops him. But according to what Syne has told him, the questions that contractors ask are easy. They want to know if the worker has experience in railway work.

He begins to cross the street at the same time that the line passes through a platform. Many mothers, wives, and children cry, scream, and throw their hands up in farewell. At first they exchange a few words, but when the foreman appears, they shut up completely. They just look at their families and eventually enter the ship.

Gregory's eyes begin to fill with tears while he waits in the office until he is seen although he has not yet made the decision to travel. Mr. Killan asks him to come in. He takes some steps, and he stops. "Come in. In Ecuador there is a president of the poor, a good person. Come." Gregory looks at the *gringo* until, in a low voice, with the last strength of his willingness, he informs him that he wants to enlist to go to work in Ecuador. Next is John Karruco, who also waited until the last moment to register because he didn't have anyone with whom to leave his family, who are in need of special care. Killan writes the names of the laborers in a booklet, in the same list that consists of Mackenzie, Spencer, Sandiford, and Taylor.

He says goodbye; and he quickly goes to a toy store and purchases a wooden cart for his son, David, and a rag doll for his daughter, Edna. The rest of money will be left to Pamela, who sells fruit on the streets.

On route, he thinks about what it will be like Ecuador. Until he reaches his home, he imagines how beautiful that country will be. He moves slowly. It would be unlikely to describe landscapes that they claim exist. He remains motionless, and in his imagination, he sees the high mountains and the very blue sky. *How wonderful!* They say that there are many birds of beautiful colors; they talk about the condor. *What is that animal like that tends to make its nest on the mountain tops and that has white chicks?* They also claim that the summits are soaring, and there is a gigantic river called the Amazon. The gold mines interest him. "With four pieces of gold, I would be rich," he thinks, "and I would buy land for the house, and I would plant sugar cane, corn . . ." He visualizes himself at the foot of the gold mine: he would sit to watch the glitter of his ingots. The contractors say that there is gold—a great deal of gold—the reason why there are no poor people in Ecuador. Lost in his thoughts, he forgets the fear of moving away from his family.

With a melancholic smile, he enters his hut. His children come out to meet him, and after giving them their toys, they jump to hug him. Gregory stops them on his chest, he holds his breath, and tears wet his cheeks. It is a kind of farewell.

The rest of the time, he does not want to speak. He understands that he will commit a serious mistake to move away from his family without taking into account that his children need him; but all of his friends came to enroll, and each time, the number of those who want to go to work in this distant country increases. At every hour, the enrollees form long lines. They are men who are jobless and come along dusty roads; they move from one end of the country to another in order to go to work in Ecuador.

Those who cannot travel due to illness or advanced age go to the port to converse with the travelers, or simply to contemplate in silence about those who are leaving the country.

But Gregory needs the money, so yes, perhaps it may be a successful journey. Immersed in his concern, he does not respond to his wife's questions; and with a breathy voice, sentence after sentence, he tells her that everything is already arranged.

That project is the magic formula to get out of poverty; he would return with money—with gold to buy the land and make their home. With these purposes, Pamela sees the advantages of the trip: she would finally have a house and land to plant in.

He prepares a sack with a shirt and patched trousers. Gregory remains silent. He looks at Pamela—who is sleeping, hugging their children. He observes them so that his heart may record their faces; then he collapses into tears with his hands on his face and tears running between his fingers, like a child crying. He watches his family with his ruthless dark eyes of tears. His wife wakes up, and they carry David and Edna to the mat where they sleep.

It is the last night they will spend together. He lifts up her skirt; she takes it over her shoulders; they blow out the lamp; it goes out; then love is turned on. They straighten up and they mess up and they dream of his happy return. He looks at his wife's face, her shiny and soft skin, her simple and pure soul with the grace of black women. He wants to observe her; he tries to guess where destiny will take her if he were missing. Fortunately, it will only be a few months that he will be in Ecuador—and time passes quickly; however, sometimes he feels lost. After a moment of hesitation, he reaffirms the convenience of moving abroad.

He wakes up meditating, but he has no other choice. He will come back with money to buy the land. He rises very slowly, and he goes to look at their children who are asleep huddled on the mat. He covers them with the sheet, and he lies down with them. He wants to listen to their breathing, to feel their warmth. It is such emotion that overwhelms him that he cannot contain his tears. He gets even closer to kiss them. He has never been so sad.

Words choke him. Something inside him produces terror and, at the same time, softens him. Gregory wants to tell them that he loves them. Instead, he spreads himself over the children. He just has the strength to think. He extends one of his arms and embraces them.

He understands that his family needs him. From that corner of his hut, the penetrating opaque light gives form to objects. Outside, the dogs bark at the moon. He smells his children's hair; he seems not to smell them with his nose but with his heart. He gets up and looks for water. He washes his face and takes some sips. When he opens his eyes well, it is still early in the morning. He goes back to the mat. He very slowly touches his wife's thigh, but she does not wake up; she is sleeping soundly. He feels her carelessly and gets even closer. She stammers something without opening her eyes, but she gently extends an arm and touches her husband's lips. Suddenly, Pamela turns around; and she awakens desire. They kiss again and again. Both seem to smile. The sound of the sea is heard. They are ships, shadow cabinetmakers—the invisible amount of echoes glimmering from the altitude or tropical outbreak.

The ship sets sail at two in the afternoon. Gregory faces the most difficult, almost impossible task: saying goodbye. He approaches his children. He picks them up in his arms, kisses them, and advises them to obey their mother. The children scream and ask him not to go while he promises to return soon. In vain he attempts to calm them. He wipes away their tears with his fingers. For them it is inexplicable; their father's trip is completely incomprehensible. *Why does he have to go so far away?* All of Gregory's explanations only accentuate the sadness.

Upon arriving at the dock, there is a lot of disorder and clamor of wives, mothers, children, siblings, and relatives of workers who are traveling to Ecuador. Some have gathered from remote places to go with them, to see them, to cry and to vent their bitterness, to reiterate to them that they love them and that they will return, and to wish them much success. They are there to offer them proof of tenderness.

Everyone is shouting at the same time; chaos grows and confusion prevails since everyone wants to talk. The travelers listen. They approve with a nod the advice that their families give them, but they also let tears escape. The children release piercing screams.

It was Sunday. For me, every Sunday smelled of beef cooked over low heat. Jenny's mother was busy placing on the table a simple cloth that at times was a tablecloth. Dad made some accounts in his notebook. Yes, I remember it exactly. It was Sunday, and it was one filled with the smell of beef cooked with wine. A damp smell reigned in the city of Kinston, and I swore to Jenny's parents to love her all her life and never to separate from her; but the lack of employment requires me to go to South America. Today she is here at the pier; she came to say goodbye. She is known for her height, and her bare shoulders shine. I strongly embrace her. She also hugs me, we cry, our and tears blend together. We look for a spot in which to knot ourselves together like snakes. I greedily kiss her. I promise her that I will come back, come back with money to build our house; then, we remain quiet and tightly embraced. I feel the heat of her body, and her heart strongly beats for us. As I move away from her, she throws herself in grieving tears. I kiss her eyes.

"I promise to return soon."

"How long?"

"I do not know, but I will come looking for you."

"And I"

"Wait for me, beautiful as always."

They smile.

"Have mercy on me, please, my full moon, and pray for me."

"I don't want you to go."

"I am carrying you in my heart. I won't forget you."

Slowly, he travels across Jenny's lips with his fingers.

"I adore you. I won't forget you, not a single moment. Wait for me. Take care of our children." He kisses her cold trembling lips.

With the first warning, the laborers are put in place and are arranged in rows. They cross the platform and accelerate their pace to get on the ship. Like a mob, the outrage of those who remain is heart-breaking. The workers raise hands over and over again to say goodbye. They push. They want to see their loved ones for the last time. And last-minute pleas and recommendations are heard. Some children faint next to their mothers. It is difficult to monitor the situation. After the boat sets sail, the crying and the screaming increase. The memories are great as they adopt new forms in promises of returning alive and healthy. They are going to South America without wanting to hear more words about not going back. Where do they draw strength to say goodbye? With bitterness, they envision the faces of their mothers, their children, their wives, their sisters. *What to do? Give up working in that beautiful land? An opportunity will not present itself again.* They would sacrifice themselves, but they would return with money for whatever they would do, except to return empty-handed.

At the insistence of Syne, Gregory is placed among a group of laborers where John Karruco is in order to say goodbye to Pamela and their children. He forces himself continually in vain to stand on tiptoe; everyone is struggling to keep themselves up front to say a last goodbye to their family. Desperately, he moves his lips with the intention of saying goodbye; but the feeling becomes stronger, and the words do not leave his mouth.

The Jamaicans embark in order to go to work—where the trees are born from some worms, and the birds are able to make nests in the sky. Proudly, they travel to provide their strength, their vigor and their youth to a brother country they are not acquainted with; and they are going to give a lesson in solidarity.

A country that Yemayá has aligned volcanoes along the high mountain ranges of stone and valleys full of butterflies and trills. What they do not know is that they are going in the capacity of slaves—only that they were not hunted as in ancient times, and instead, they leave voluntarily to collaborate with their heroic efforts, knowledge, and experience.

The boat moves slowly away. The foreman speaks to them in order to calm tempers. The boats have sailed throughout the month. They should carry four thousand laborers. Ships seem to be small for the number of those who will go.

The nature of the crew ignites easily; violence can produce a crisis that needs to be handled with great care. In the course of hours, a period of relative calm occurs; and despite the discomfort and tightness in the traveling, each one looks for a place to situate himself. Some laborers show their disagreement. Now they doubt the type of work they will undertake. By calculating the consequences, it is Syne who reassures his companions and ensures them that the *gringos* will pay four *reales* daily and will treat them well; however, doubts persist.

They travel and travel while Gregory cannot resign himself. He will not let it enter in his head the benefit that he will get out of leaving his family, and a bitter disappointment begins to invade him. He stands up and goes in search of a more convenient location. That is what happens—changing his place. He knits his eyebrows, and his lips whisper incomprehensible words while he watches the sea.

In between those changes, Gregory is isolated. His traveling companions talk, ask questions, and express interest in knowing what Ecuador will be like. They ask questions without stopping. When Gregory is looking for another place, he meets a teenager who takes a step to give him a seat. His name is Lamboreo Balket. They begin to tell each other many things about their lives. Lamboreo is orphaned from a father and a mother. He grew up with his maternal grandmother, but she also died before the arrival of the contractors; and that was his reason for enrolling on the trip. He is optimistic in finding a better future. Marret, after appreciating the teenager's joy, is no longer thinking negatively; and he acquires a new orientation. He understands that the boy, being a child, thinks with faith and with an extraordinary optimism; and he feels the need to experience new challenges. He considers what a good job it is to work on the railway line and to get acquainted with the magnificent project in South America. Gregory believes that young people manage to better understand and do not stop themselves to express their satisfaction of traveling by sea. They enjoy new experiences; they feel the need to do and undo, open and fulfill adventures, establish and modify the rules of the game of life. That perpetual desire for action is the very nature of the activity.

On the contrary, Gregory expresses fear. Perhaps it is only a sense of his having left his family alone; however, he would risk everything to succeed.

The eyes of the authorities from Ecuador will be keeping an eye on the work that the Jamaicans do so that, even in their dreams, they would not misbehave. His thoughts are interrupted because it is his turn at the mess hall for a meal consisting of a fruit, a piece of bread with cheese and water.

The workers look for a place to accommodate themselves in. While they eat, the murmur ceases; then they exchange words. No one rejects anyone; everyone is accepted as they are. All have a single goal—to work and to return with money—and in this way, a brotherhood is formed.

They quietly exchange impressions. They always find an opportunity to meet someone to share concerns and express their needs, and in this way, they relieve tensions. They breathe sweating. They show kindness and generosity toward their companions; that is the first contact between them. They forget the place from which they come, and they strive to achieve a brotherhood.

Overwhelmed by poverty, destitution, or any other misfortune, they have responded to the call because of the lack of employment in their country. Nothing seems difficult or impossible to them when it comes to helping someone who is in need; everyone is aware of their companion's health.

During the evenings, those who are in the ship's hold climb up and go on deck to watch the starry sky; those who can hide their dreams fall asleep, but there are many who are not in the mood to sleep.

They are in agreement on many details. In that atmosphere of goodwill, laborers take turns on places on the boat; however, the signs of tiredness pop up everywhere, and gradually they sink under the fatigue. At irregular intervals, foremen are present to monitor the laborers.

The people long to arrive soon. Every day they look, in the middle of a cloudy morning, at the horizon. Unconsciously, they contemplate the sea and the foam; and nostalgia begins. They no longer feel encouraged, and those who were talkative during conversations are mute. The memory of their relatives and of Jamaica comes as something great, dear, and close. They are linked to that set of adventures that they have to deal with and must overcome, or they suffer like one big family. This experience is an intimate bond between all those who have been enlisted to work in the Andes. They have the obligation to feel strongly unified by memories of their homeland.

That same night, a dense rain falls, the wind whips the boat, and a thick haze covers the sea. Because of the storm, it begins to produce panic. The ship loses direction and, without finding the route, comes to a halt. Everything is vague and strange. The crew suspects that something is wrong; the sway of the boat is strong, and with each wave, it rises in order to fall violently. In such circumstances, the authorities fear a mutiny. The roughness with which the waves smash makes the water penetrate the deck.

The guards express concern; they are ready to respond to emergencies. They make the men spread out throughout the ship in order to maintain the balance. A group unleashes a cry and makes a gesture with their hands. They demand that they tell them what is happening. Other groups mutter isolated and incomprehensible words, but there is no doubt they are words of rejection.

They begin to describe tales and stories about the large number of shipwrecks to each other; they find a bitter pleasure at the prospect that the trip may fail without hope of salvation. The grumblings are mixed with legends that are known among the people of the region.

In those circumstances, the laborers easily invent sea adventures; and fear spreads rapidly. Unconsciously, Lamboreo Balket sneaks away; he doesn't want to hear such stories of ghosts and drowning. He pretends that he is going to look out of a window, but it is impossible; and finally fear enters.

He goes in search of Syne, who is curious about a rather strange laborer; so he remains at the bottom of the boat and experiences a few moments of bitterness. He meets Hugh Spencer, who is feeling his friend's eyes riveted on the torn football shirt that he is wearing. He tells him, "It's for us to enjoy playing football." Balket quickly says goodbye.

Everyone is desperate to arrive and to start work as quickly as possible so they can soon return to their country. During the afternoon of that day (that endless afternoon, that loud and warm afternoon), the crew talks loudly. It would seem that they want to waste their energy on something or that they want something else; they would like others to know where they come from, or what is it that triggers their desire to gain importance in front of their peers. They talk about their knowledge and skills in railroad work and worry some about themselves. In the end, they ask themselves, what is happiness? It is nothing but a continuing effort to create it. The crews feel capable of doing the work that will be recommended to them. Optimism, the thought of their spirit, is to leave the name of Jamaica high.

They vote on intentions. Nothing indicates that they are afraid of heights, of the depths, and of insects that will eventually conquer their resistance and will take them to their death. They travel sure that they will be successful. They notice the pleasure of collaborating with a brother country; and according to Mister Killan, there exists in the Ecuador a very honest and simple ruler, a very kind man. The Jamaicans make the decision to comply with their duties and be supportive.

Implicit in that is the fact of the amazing feats that they will have to fulfill to honor their country. Gregory watches Lamboreo with excitement; the boy seems very brave. His black eyes shine, and with delicate attention, he listens to the advice of the Marret brothers. He seems satisfied when Syne is at times like a father.

The crew smiles when the storm moves away, and they take the opportunity to observe the strange figure of the laborer. While the authorities raise their eyebrows, it seems incredible to them that the trip may have developed successfully. The friendly talk of the laborers becomes a dialogue; they talk effortlessly, with unexpected satisfaction, about things that they have never said before. Some express a mixture of seriousness in referring to their legends and tales, which they say are true. They also defend their ideas about the origin of the universe. When they talk, they try to express their ideas through myths. For them, it is more accurate to formulate their beliefs in that way.

Legends are not invented; they are real facts and are filled with emotions that they respect and love and that deeply penetrate the flesh.

Everything is historic; they had occurred at one time. Some excessively encompass sorrows of reality while others repeat the yearning for freedom.

They have always existed, of course, in a close relationship with the community and the environment. But this relationship is even more striking with words—which the elders tell their children and their grandchildren not only on moonlit nights or on free hours or upon displays of enthusiasm and the suffering of the heart or during discussions of which poverty was the cause, but that on a daily basis, for hours and days, sweetly counting with the soul, or just contemplating the landscape, they do not lose the vocation of narrating such words. The fate of the country is sung through them.

They imagine numerous romantic plots, multiple scenes of abuse, and racial passions in these legends. Never—not even with the generational change—do they forget them. That day and others, until the arrival in port, the laborers begin to sing on the boat in chorus. The authorities come out strolling through the cargo hold, stopping in front of the laborers, laughing, sharing a whim. The person who seems like a picture of illness is immediately separated to avoid contagion.

That activity and that energy that characterize the Jamaican people are magnificent qualities for the work which they will perform in Ecuador. It is very interesting and surprising to discover that these are men of public action and workers with clear ideas.

The contractors are impressed by the remarkable behavior of those recruited; that wonderful joy is beneficial in order to work, and they are persons who rapidly escape from sadness and discouragement. Precisely because of that enthusiasm and sweetness, they do not allow more than a footprint of happiness and joy on their soul.

The miraculous musicality that the laborers demonstrate seems to surge in them; they are attentive to the joys of a miraculous paradise, which the contractors cannot understand. The workers chat loudly, laugh, applaud, sing, recite, and even shout with excitement. Daily they express their satisfaction and wait, longing for the moment of landing; and they always go back to that feeling of superhuman joy, which is an invisible wall that separates them.

Despite fatigue, Gregory feels happy to go along with Syne—with his attractive face, dark eyes, and rosy looks—and with Lamboreo, who is always ready for action and with the desire to serve. He runs from one side to another helping those suffering from dizziness. Gregory rubs his hands at the thought that his wife and their children are together playing with the wooden car and the doll that he gave them. He looks at the horizon, now bright with absolute clarity, under blue, yellow, and violet rays. He looks at everything and approves of it all. He says to himself that he will return with money to buy the land.

The contractors very kindly salute and smile at the laborers. At times, they pat this or that enlisted man on the shoulder. They carefully go up and down the stairs and agree to talk with everyone; and this contact makes the journey less burdensome. They motivate them in order to animate them. Even for the *gringos,* the music that the Jamaicans sing is unintelligible; and they remember that they have a responsibility to arrive with workers ready to make President Alfaro's project a success.

Mr. H. Killan's head hurts, but he doesn't notice his discomfort; rather, he gratefully looks at the Jamaicans. He is wearing blue pants and a short sleeved shirt. He is very tall, and traces of the sun loom in his face. He behaves himself unceremoniously and is always attentive to the direction of the ship. He asks the captain to go faster to shorten the days of the trip, but it is impossible for him to obey.

The captain regularly advises him about the state in which the ship moves, and the *gringos* show interest in assessing the conditions facing the sea. All authorities work, examining, planning, and tracking the statuses; they want no detail to escape in order to tell don Eloy. They establish a list of those who are traveling although it is impossible to identify them. But they look carefully at a passenger who is different from the others since he has a less pronounced arch of the eyebrows, his forehead is smaller, and his hands have elongated fingers. His voice is completely different from his peers. He is the same person Syne has been observing, and that draws attention to his lively eyes.

It is Leona Cuebute—who, covered with a blanket and wearing pants, has embarked in the direction of Ecuador. She believes that no one suspects her boldness and that nobody will discover that she is a woman, which is why no one notices her presence. Everything she sees and everything she hears is a secret to her. If she is discovered—may Yemayá not allow it!—they would throw her in the sea. She does not dare to think about sharing her story, but she hears someone calling her. She feigns not to listen; nevertheless, Syne approaches her. She turns her face and hides it in the blanket.

"Hey, what is your name? Why are you so thoughtful?" Up to this moment, Leona has not thought about changing her name. Being asked for the second time, her black eyes dilate; and a few of the whitest teeth appear. For Syne, it is a question to a thin young man with a woman's smile. They look directly at each other, both smile, and they think about each other in admiration—the first impulse to be known. Syne does not manage to see her face since she covers it while she is quiet, but those ardent black eyes impress him.

"My name is Syne Marret, and you?"

"León Cuebute."

A few moments of silence follow. She continues immobile; she is not very sure if she wants to strike up a friendship with Syne, but she is anxious to talk with someone. She does not say a word. She is exhausted, has menstruated, and cannot sleep. Marret says goodbye and moves away.

In the boat, the heat and the fatigue cause havoc. Many laborers have taken off their shirt; she sees that they are strong. This strength is observed in the chest, shoulders, and back that shine with perspiration. Leona looks for another place to rest. The trip turns out to be difficult for her, but she thinks that her life will be very good in Ecuador. She is alone in the world since her mother has become engaged with a man who was not her father, and she decided to make her life far away. The construction of the railway line is a good opportunity to triumph. She can cook, wash, iron, and foresee luck in a glass of water; she would defend herself in any trade. She does not regret having boarded, for in the hamlet where she was living, there was a lot of poverty. Now she is looking for new horizons, but to leave means to break with everything that is hers—her own being. Sometimes she wonders why her region is so poor.

She remembers that—on having left her village—while the whitest mist rose out of the sea. A veil was covering her face. The hamlet was transformed by a magical spell of sadness before the setting of the sun. Her hamlet, her beloved land, will live inside her forever. She abandoned her hut without saying goodbye to anybody, which is why she did not want to erase her footprints. She only felt like getting to the port. Nevertheless, she turned to study her hamlet, to see it for the last time with admiration. There she had been born, had grown up; and her mother was still there. She never looked at it in this way. The fear of the future attacked her, and her nostalgia is entirely justified. For her, without money, existence was not easy; but she will demonstrate to herself her capacity to fight and that life is good. She is ready to accept any challenge. She wants to succeed, to live in better conditions—and the opportunity has presented itself—because being a woman and black was not going to allow her to escape. She would fight with all her strength to adapt herself to the circumstances.

Her village had the face of poverty, but she would always remember it with love even if it were only for that poverty. "Soon we will come to Ecuador. I will return with money, and I cannot allow myself to carry either nostalgia or despondency," she was thinking. The idea would make her collapse. She looks at the enlisted men, their arms, and their chests. They are young, robust, and beautiful; then she notices their hands. They are healthy and strong. She happily smiles. She has health and beauty, and she desires to work without thinking about what she may have to do. The question is to have a job, a trade. She gets up, moves between a group of laborers, and stumbles over Syne, who takes her by the arm when he sees that his friend is losing his balance. Quickly she thanks him and moves forward. She turns, stops, contemplates the faces of her traveling partners; they all have the look of anxiety. She moves back to a corner, where she thinks about the future in which she will live.

The bosses are giving special provisions for the program that will develop when they disembark in the next port; they believe that it is necessary for the crew to leave the ship in order to repair it since it has suffered a small breakdown with the storm and, at the same time, so that the laborers can get some sun and stretch their legs. The contractors need for everyone to arrive in good, healthy condition and for an epidemic not to break out.

With the damage repaired, the laborers climb back onboard in the same precipitation with which they went down; and Leona listens as they call her. It is Syne, who is waiting to sit down next to her. Her heart is pounding. She wishes that she could tell him why she is going to Ecuador to work. She has not just imagined that she has received a miracle because, from that moment on, she will not separate from that man. She is curious to get to know him well, and she is happy to find a friend to confess to him that she is a woman.

It is all that Leona thinks about while they share an orange that Syne offers to her. They listen to loud voices, laughs, and screams. The discussion is a sign that they are set to work with great determination.

There are many moments of good humor among the Jamaicans; they do not cultivate bad habits or resentment, and their state of mind is not insincere. Those moments reveal optimism, a cheerful spirit; they are sure that they will return healthy and unharmed.

They all are determined to return to Jamaica; this thought helps them to calm their anxiety, and they all support each other with the strength of their unconditional certainties. Syne Marret possesses a special energy, an extraordinary capacity of a leader with an unbreakable faith united to action.

He organizes the workers, speaks to them, cheers them up during the following days. He talks with the representatives of the company. He has experience in railroad construction; nevertheless, the work circumstances on the construction of the South Railroad are different because of the climate, the altitude, and the food. A constant ebb and flow of questions are done in search of something that they cannot define with certainty.

To work on the railway line makes them enthusiastic, and they feel the need to know the details about the country and to know the characteristics of the region. For them, changing the world does not mean losing their identity but a personal transformation on having put into practice their customs and, perhaps, having modified their world view. The environment in which they develop their activities will serve to reaffirm them individually, to acquire new experiences, or perhaps to become a kind of straight line that has no end. They are ready to be foreigners capable of receiving and assimilating the Ecuadorian spirit and of demonstrating their skill and discipline.

Fatigue begins to cause damages; their bones and muscles hurt from being seated for so long. The slowness of the ship frightens them, and they give in to sleep on the floor. Some of the laborers have strolled from one side to the other for more than four years with the mission to contribute their strength for the construction of these long snakes of iron, and each time, they acquire new knowledge.

The company representatives do not want to speak a word about the real situation that will touch the Jamaicans' lives. With serious faces, they inform them that a railroad will be constructed to join two regions: the coast and the mountain range. It is clear that on having answered the laborers' questions, they answer that this country, Ecuador, is located in the middle of the world, that it has two climates, and that the people are very good. Having spoken and rubbing his hands, Mr. Killan understands that the Jamaicans, with the greatest innocence in the world, trust them.

They are anxious to arrive. They are sweaty and anxious to populate these places where, according to what the contractors have told them, the stars serve as a guide; and they wonder what the Andes will be like. Leona has made herself a friend in Lamboreo Balket, Syne, Gregory, Mackenzie, Spencer, Sandiford, and John Karruco, who tell histories while he re-enacts the facts as they all laugh. Leona, nervous and shy, coughs with a dry short cough that she does not realize. Her friends observe her, amused. Syne, to whom she looks like a special person, has his eyes fixed on her. Leona thinks that when they discover her real identity, she will have to flee. She knows that her friends will whisper "How rude!" In this way, she would finish her adventure. She would look for employment in some big house.

After saying goodbye, she advances toward the ship's hold. She moves closer to the wall to fall asleep. The trip turns out to be long for her, and she is bored with nothing to do. She needs to take off her pants, but she cannot. When she has little time before they arrive, she has only to manage as she can; and growing weak, she puts her hand on her genital area. In these moments, with so much nervousness, the blood is profusely coming down. She is afraid that if they discover it, they could throw her into the sea. In a few hours, she will arrive to Ecuador; and she has to remain healthy. Ecuador, according to the laborers, is a magical place, where vegetation spills onto the ground so that everything blooms—that the moon is so big that it looks like a lamp, that the sky is blue (but a good blue) that it almost seems painted. How astonishing!

Nobody told them that in those landscapes, God shows His strong, severe face and that He planted the Tree of Life. That when the Andes snatch Him from His jail of solitude and burrow into His blue prison, He feels cosmic anguish; then He unleashes His wrath. The real stone awakens from its dream, and when a few intruders want to divulge the most ancient news, His voice trembles with courage; and they will see arms, heads, and bodies flying through the air. It is the prophecy of the Andes.

The workers feel knocked down by the heat and the discomfort. The illusion or the reality that they are suffering is the beginning of a series of inconveniences that they will have to face.

The debate has been stopped (that feverish activity has ceased). Subdued faces, with closed eyes, resistance gives way to weariness. In spite of her intense fatigue, Leona sees a ray of light. Occasionally, she raises her head to observe her companions. She wonders, *What a coincidence it is to have embarked on the same ship as Syne.* With him things would be simplified. The Marret brothers and Lamboreo mention that León wears his pants too big, which he has to hold up with a rope. He looks like a fat person because he seems gathered on all sides. His looks and his voice reveal something strange to them, and she strains to remain entertaining in order to make them believe that she is like the others.

Years ago, Leona came to accept with resignation her mother's absence; and she observes her companions' happiness when they talk about their relatives. *How Gregory's words and gestures transform him when he talks about his children and Pamela!* Leona feels the need to listen to this happiness that her friend experiences. For a moment, Lamboreo remains thoughtful. He does not have anybody to remember, and he will never have. He will always feel that emotional gap that the absence of his parents left in him; that's why he needs his friends. He knows that he cannot sink into sadness. He must be successful, and he wants to be an example for other adolescents. He needs support to achieve his intention. For that reason, he sows friendship with the Marret brothers and with León.

At night the weather changes: a cold wind enters, and in a few hours, the sky becomes blue and cloudless. The wind blows strongly, getting under the clothing. The laborers cover their faces with their hands and curl up. Lamboreo's face is protected with a rag, and with an apologetic air, he avoids the cold. Leona tries to maintain her calm. She discreetly covers her ears and stops listening to the wind that is striking the boat. Sometimes she wonders what the mystery is that exists in nature: Where does the wind come from? And what are the clouds made of? And why does the sea have waves? But her companions do not have the answers to these questions either. She remains calm and polite. For her, anything alien to the concrete world is incomprehensible. *How was it possible that the sea waved and had that musicality and profound happiness that accompanied the fish, and precisely with this musicality, the animals were happy?* Yes, they were very happy. "Could anybody exist the entire day agitating the waters of the immense sea? It is impossible to believe that the wind will be the one that makes the swells," she said to herself. She feels that her breathing is less rapid, and she manages to calm down. She lifts her face and smiles at Syne. "He is not an ugly young man. I like him." This will be her new family; they will allow her to find a better situation upon arriving to Ecuador, which is essential. This attitude in her is born of the need to be protected, to be respected, and to avoid clashes and confrontations. Feeling alone makes her panic, a sensation that is growing; it leaves her breathless. She intuitively senses any circumstance that could spoil her peace of mind. On the one hand, she is afraid of being the only woman in the camp. In such a case, she would have to draw strength to be respected. She would have to discover among so many men one that was distinctive.

She pays attention to what they are announcing. She pretends that she is not afraid of anything or anybody. When tears fill her eyes, she quickly hides her face in order not to be discouraged. She remembers her mother. The memory hurts her soul, but erasing that nostalgia is inevitable; then, she is filled with happiness as a legacy of her race, the starting point of her genes, a thread that unravels—or a long chain that although it breaks, returns to unite her ties. Certainly, the idea of having left her mother and finding herself alone gives her the ability to recognize a persistent determination. From that bewilderment of being and not being, she manages to get up and fly again in the perspective of a new opportunity. It would be the culmination of all these years of hoping. It oppresses her heart to glance at the faces of the enlisted men. They are all going around with the same worry, in a certain way; and they will face an unknown society. They accepted the work because of the way the contractors presented the proposition. Their kindness was doubly refreshing, after the personal interest of constructing a railroad in Ecuador, a beautiful country. Also, their commitments to General Eloy Alfaro made their sense of respect toward him strengthen their arguments; and with this logic, they tried to enroll the largest number of laborers.

Next to Leona is Gregory, to whom it seems ingenuous to travel that far. He continues to consider it stupid to have left his family to look for wealth. He feels annoyed and impatient, and he begins to question his own optimism and to wonder if he really will return with money. Somewhat disconcerted, he feels that the situation which he is in (traveling) is not the most appropriate. He observes Lamboreo's eyes. His eyes are so vivacious and alert. Gregory momentarily feels a shudder. He cowardly notices; then, when his pessimism is greater, seeds of hope are produced. He thinks that his name will appear among those who worked on the railway and that the people of Ecuador will receive them with bands of people and that someday his children will read a plaque that will say "We pay homage to Gregory Marret, hero." They will feel proud of their father. It produces comfort in him to think that. He has always boasted of being a good, qualified, and strong worker; it would be great if his name were recorded in the train station in Quito. He makes an effort not to get up and jump for joy.

In truth, the images of victory have been spontaneously appearing before him. Compared to this yearning, he believes that it is wonderful to take that work as his own. He believes in the contractors' word that "they would have a good salary and good treatment." Gregory finds himself in a state of effervescence that he already perceives the imagined as having occurred.

The expression on his face changes. He looks at his brother Syne with his eyes that express an immense joy; he feels that the Jamaicans' success is a reality. This awakens new energies, and the weariness passes him. He notes the advantages of the contract. He is satisfied—everybody should be. This is the most important fact in the history of the workers in his country. The contractors say that there are no dangers, that all will return safely. Gregory straightens up, invaded by a wave of satisfaction and of happiness; the idea of succeeding has piqued an interest in him of what the work will be like. A long time of experience enables them to perform successfully. They are skillful on the railway line, and they are updated on laying rails. He is already listening to the laughter of satisfaction of the engineers who will tell him, "Magnificent! Very well done, Greg!" At the end of the assignment, they will give him good food and good drink, which is something wonderful. At the end of the week, he will lie down to rest all day. He will pompously be glad to listen to the mister praise his performance. "You are a first-class worker!"

The anguish and the crazy adventure to move away from the family will have their reward: it is his name that is going to become engraved in the stone as an example of heroism. They will have to write the name of Gregory Marret well. He arches his eyebrows. He is convinced that the contractors would make the list of the heroes. He observes Lamboreo and asks him if he has another name. "Yes, my grandmother called me Aniceto. Aniceto Balket. But call me Lamboreo."

Facing these deep thoughts, Gregory imagines scenes in which a crowd around the Jamaicans hail them as heroes of Ecuador.

CHAPTER TWO

On November 29, 1900, the Jamaican laborers arrive at the port of the Guayas province. Divided into crews, they navigate up the river until reaching Durán; then, they advance toward the mountainous region. There they raise the first camp and give it the name of *Olimpo*; and the other one, they name *Nido de Águila* (Eagle's nest)—perhaps to frighten the shadows of the weather since only the radiance of the eagle-eyed perception remains.

Having gone to the designated site, Lamboreo looks at the abyss; then, he raises his glance toward the sky. He is pale. And he, to whom everything gives a touch of happiness, suddenly feels a fear that makes him tremble. "Oh! What a deep abyss! What a dangerous cliff!" He crosses himself on having seen it. Worried, he seems to abandon the hope that is, undoubtedly, the hope of all the Jamaicans: to return alive.

The laborers worriedly observe the abyss that quietly attracts them like a magnet. It resembles an animal that is sniffing rumps. It throws out a so-called sound and has empty eyes. They believe that the abyss makes a mockery of everyone. It raises a mist in a defiant attitude. Conceited, it thirsts for shade and solitude. It wants to triumph in all of its ambushes. They move away with panting breath and leave with a dizzying fear. They follow with the gaze of the flying condor, on the other side are the tall mountains—so high and majestic that they stand up straight like stone warriors.

The Andes, monarchs of an empire frozen in time, resemble the return from some extraterrestrial travel and are firmly bound by the beauty of the Earth.

Everything on the summit is exciting. There is a hurricane of stars, and the workers meditate with the biggest eyes that they have. They consider the experience of being in those places a privilege: for them, it constitutes a mysterious and sinister landscape although it's of unusual beauty, the heart of the Andes. They are invisible beings raised in the air.

The laborers call out. They long for the past that they shared with their families, when they embraced their children. They close their eyes and stop time. Silence invades everything. They only listen to their own memories; sometimes it seems that these memories have ceased to belong to them. How they walk and work in a mechanical mind. How the blood of their bodies is no longer in their arteries. It is something completely strange. Their thoughts belong to another time. They are forced to adapt themselves to that monstrous place, which might be the "promised land." It is a paradox that leads them to reflect.

The Trans-Andean Railroad will be a pleasure for the country, but the workers do not have anybody to assume the responsibility for the mishaps that they will suffer. They are enlisted in the service of a cause that is not theirs; nevertheless, in spite of themselves, they are ready to sacrifice themselves to the service of Ecuador.

The ambiguity of this situation in which they are immersed—devotion and sacrifice, illness and death—leads them to wondering if it is possible to take a step backward. There is nothing more difficult, nothing more than to affirm that it is a benefit for the sister country and for Alfaro. They will demonstrate their feelings without taking into account if the task is dangerous.

The catastrophic situation that crosses the railroad is the reason why nobody wants to work, and the lack of labor could ruin the gigantic project. They forget the tensions, and because of this insight, they believe in the singular and illuminating plan of destiny. They have committed to work until they finish the railroad. They will demonstrate solidarity although they do not know if they will return alive. They are going to fight against the abysses, the sun beams, the winters, the sunburns, the landslides, the winds, the altitude sicknesses, and the insects.

The torrential rains make the situation more difficult. They need to adopt a position of dignity and of honor in order not to desert. History will not be able to accuse them of having come to Ecuador as elusive and unsympathetic men.

One of the crews consists of Syne (who is the leader), Gregory, Mackenzie, Sandiford, Spencer, Taylor, Lamborero, Leona, and John Karruco, among others who usually eat in the sitting room of doña Miche, who has a seventeen-year-old daughter. They are proud to have been working long before the sun came out. It is the daily routine. They form a long line to receive a drink of brandy that has macerated roots and flowers that have healing properties against malaria.

In the sitting room, doña Miche and her daughter, Luisa, serve them a chicken broth with yucca, banana, *chiyangua*[4], and a little rice. Every Sunday, the proprietress prepares the railroad rice.

This Sunday, Michael Sandiford and Syne Marret throw a ball up to reach the top of a wall. This way, they are entertained until they call them to lunch. Luisa is in the kitchen and leaves her face partially shaded. Suddenly, she lifts her skirt to dry her hands off; and she exposes her thighs. Michael, on having seen her, feels burning desire: a strong wish and an impulse drag him toward the young woman who, with her rhythmic gait and her thin and toasted face, emits a breath of beauty.

Michael closes his eyes, trying to remember Jenny's image; but it is deleted, and that image of Luisa appears again before his eyes, so animated and so real. He listens to her sing, a bloody upheaval shakes him, and his face burns. It is his Jenny that flutters like a sparrow between the leaves.

---

[4] *Chiyangua* is a condiment found primarily on the Pacific coast of Colombia and Ecuador.

He listens to Luisa's singing; all of her is musical. He half-closes his eyes, and he listens to her with his heart. "No, Yemayá, help me. I have to return to Kinston. Jenny is waiting for me," he says to himself.

Luisa's singing distracts him; it impels him to imagine her undressed, and that aromatic body begins to torture him. She smiles at him. She is good with him; she always serves him a large portion of rice or adds an empanada, and she sits down next to him. Michael does not know what to do; no human force is capable of restraining her. "Luisa is a prohibited fruit. I have my Jenny," he says to himself, and he recalls:

From the outside, Michael sees the burners go out. He waits impatiently on the other side of the fence. He conceals his anxiety by whistling and has a fixed look on Jenny's parents' house, which is often confused in the darkness of the night. His dates with the young woman are increasingly more difficult.

He waits for the girl to come out. In the village, they say that Jenny's father is very strict, that he had come from an island located across from Jamaica, that he possessed a plot of land in the mountains, and that when he decided to have a family, he purchased a house in Kinston.

After the light of the burner goes out, Jenny comes out to meet Michael, who trembles with excitement on seeing his *Luna Llena*.

"I have told you not to call me that."

"It is not my fault."

"Why do you say that to me?"

"Well," he says thoughtfully, "because you are a light that enchants clarity . . . you are the light of my life."

They laugh.

One Sunday, at the start of the afternoon, the lovers turn up at Jenny's parents' home to inform them that they are going to get married. In the environment, the smell of veal cooked with wine and carrots circulates.

"I advise you to leave and right now!"

"I have done my duty. I love your daughter."

"Father, let me marry Michael."

"No, you are very young."

"I love your daughter. Please understand."

"You will leave her."

"I will never, ever. I swear it."

That Sunday, a few young people are playing with a ball in a court in front of Jenny's house. Michael greets a tall and thin young man named Hugh Spencer. This Sunday, Jenny's house smells of veal stewed with wine; and for Michael, every Sunday has the smell of veal cooked with wine.

Now, in Ecuador, he recalls:

"I got married. We went to spend our honeymoon on her father's farm. No, there was no noise, only the warble of the birds. It was a Sunday, and Jenny was bathing on the flat roof. I saw her take off her dress. She was not wearing a bra. Having seen her breasts, I was tempted to run to kiss them, but I continued looking at her enraptured, mute. The full moon was reflecting on the humble roof."

They demand more and more work, obedience, and discipline. The control is very strict while the conditions in which the tasks are operated are difficult: the climate is very humid, the rains do not stop being torrential, and they accentuate the dangers. There is no safety in the work. The authorities prove to be impatient when the laborers fall ill. Often the people disappear, and no other explanation exists than death although this is not part of the agreement. What to do if now they cannot leave the job? If they refuse to keep on working to raise the iron line, they would ruin don Eloy's work.

It calls to their attention the important fact that sometimes they receive praises from the great Harman, who admires the maneuvers and skill of the black Jamaicans. Suddenly, the fear of disappointing Harman comes to them; and they make efforts to earn the praises.

Gradually they are introduced, more and more, in the thickness of the jungle. They open trails crossed by innumerable currents that grow with the rains. Rain falls endlessly from a gray sky that looks more like a dark mirror through which colorful birds fly. Nearby the roaring of wild animals is heard. Syne's crew gets in line like a long snake that slowly breaks up writhing. The workers take spades, hammers, spikes, axes, and machetes; and they begin the work of dismantling the mountain where the rails will be.

They feel the rustling of the fallen trees. The air smells like innocent sap, and it sounds like a flute that is weeping. The trees moan and the mountain suffocates with the crying. The leaves roll in turmoil; and the birds, dazed with fear, chirp incessantly as they discover that they have lost their green paradise. It disturbs the fragrant air of the resin and extends its ladder of crying. It is necessary to raise twenty-five bridges, and it is necessary to tear down a big part of the forest.

Lamboreo's desires are many; and he sadly looks at Leona, who lacks the strength to drag the tree pieces. These adolescents do not want to convince themselves that the railroad will slide, crossing the smell of the dead poplars that saturates the wind of flight. It is useless; nobody stops to clear the route, and they all regularly continue their work. Leona casts a frightened look around her; she is afraid that the guardian of the jungle, *El Bambero*, will punish them.[5] One only hears a long lament and the drunken noise of the birds when they toss their nests down with their chicks inside.

At midday, the workers are called so that they can serve themselves bread with cheese accompanied by some fruit and water. Leona knows that any minute now, the Bambero will appear; and it will begin its revenge. Syne laughs at her bright ideas and observes her with admiration since for him, Leona each day invents a new happiness as if she were getting up early to have a breakfast of stars. For him, this adolescent is in fact a woman because he smells the perfume of her hormones on the surface of her skin and because once he discovered blood in her urine. He was silent about what he discovered.

The following day, at the moment of knocking it down, a tree fell down on a few workers and killed one. And since then, the misfortunes

---

[5] El Bambero is an Afro-Ecuadorian mythical character with no physical form that is a protective spirit of jungle animals. According to its imposed law man can kill animals to feed on the condition that the hunter must abandon wounded and suffering. If the hunter does not, he must bear the same conditions of the suffering animal. The hunter can break free from the penalty by taking the beloved animal home.

(Taken from: *Popular Culture in Ecuador*, Volume IV, Esmeraldas, 2nd. Edition, IV-1996, Research coordinator: Marcelo Naranjo, Central American Crafts and Folk Art, CIDAP).

come. Leona reflects, tries to remove the bad thoughts; but she has no doubts. The guardian of the jungle has initiated its revenge.

She follows orders. She cannot escape from the work, which is increasingly heavier and more difficult. While she remains in the camp, her worry is to be discovered in her real identity. Generally, she works along with Lamboreo. They drag branches, gather sheets and stones, and carry sleeping cots. It is all under the terrible sun that sears the workers' bodies.

The work of the Southern Railroad, which was at a standstill in Chimbo, is reactivated by the management headed by don Eloy Alfaro and the businessman Archer Harman. The latter is nearly fifty years old. He is tall, blond, and with an impressive appearance and strong character. The laborers call him Mister Tomato because his cheeks are always red. He is a very active person; he has formed a shareholders' trade union, among which are the engineer and Economist Edward Morley.

Archer Harman and Edward Morley had arrived to the city of Milagro, not to Guayaquil because it was still almost in ruins as a result of the voracious fire that, in 1896, devastated many apples, and because of the presence of yellow fever. They make use of the railway to Chimbo, from where they continue on mule back to Pallantanga-Cajabamba. They, then, take the wagon to Quito. They waste five days on the trip. It is the first time that they travel by a mule and the first that they hear the trill of so many birds, listening with pleasure. The variety of landscapes and climates is amazing. They are happy to see the Andes. Edward Morley calculates the value of these lands when the railroad crosses those territories. As an economist, he knows that he can do a good business; but he does not communicate this to Mister Harman because he knows of his sternness and his honesty.

General Alfaro is aware of the importance of the interview, and Harman and Morley know that they are going to meet the great leader and statesman; that is why they are living exciting moments, without bubbles or protocols, when they interview and get along with don Eloy. "El Viejo Luchador" and shareholders mutually present their respects and desire to build the railway. A higher spirit unites don Eloy and Harman, who have a lot of confidence in each other. For Alfaro, both professionals have ability, experience, and—above all—capacity of grandiose dreams; and dreams for him are manifested in the effort to reach the goal.

The shareholders are amazed. They had not expected anything like that to exist in a small country like Ecuador, an atmosphere with the tenacity of a lion; the will and royal personality of Alfaro is obvious to them, and they promise to continue the work on the Trans-Andean Railroad as don Eloy calls it.

They insist on their word of honor in order to reach a general understanding about the basis of the contract, which is going to start without a penny. The price of the work amounted to twelve million and two hundred eighty-two thousand *sucres*, which should be covered with bonds, at 6% interest and 1% depreciation. It reinforces The Guayaquil and Quito Railway Company and starts their activities with the repair on the existing railway at the same time widening the line from 36 to 42 inches from Chimbo North, for which they need to bring in the Jamaican laborers.

The crew composed of the Marret brothers and others is here to carry out an inspection to clear the land where the railway line will pass. They are surprised because as they enter the peaks, the ground increasingly slips away; and the task they perform is a failure.

They have done this kind of work before, in another, more stable type of soil. They really think that it is a bad idea to continue that work; another way must be followed since the soil cannot bear the weight of the railway. All are in agreement that the situation is very difficult. They work for two weeks, and then the workers ask themselves if it is necessary to communicate the situation to Mister Harman; however, they fear bothering him with so many problems and observations which all require him to resolve. But if they do not report the change to him, they are the ones who could endanger the railway line. They understand that the news will be unpleasant, so they decide to communicate to Henry Davis, the engineer who designed the plan. The crew stops to tell him what they have observed: not only is the earth fragile, but so are the course of the water, wind, weather, and erosion. While the laborers try to widen the road, the ground recedes as it receives blows from the picks and the blades.

Leona cleans her hands on her pants. It is the fifth or seventh time that she makes the gesture. She does not know why she does it. Her hands are swollen and they hurt. They have worked since the first hours of the day, and they have empty stomachs. They do not have permission to rest either, and the day ends at dusk. Other crews arrive at that time. The only liquid that they have is rainwater. They have to continue opening the road in large tracts of the forest, which makes the trail impassable. From time to time, flocks of birds of various colors emerge from the vegetation.

One afternoon, they are surprised by a huge snake that sinks its fangs into the legs of several laborers. Screams and cries rise up, and there is no way to establish order. The shouting occurs as if the crowd were going to save the wounded, lying on the grass. They shudder in pain. Everyone expresses fear, they chase the animal, and words of hate can be heard (accompanied by a shower of stones). They cut the grass from the thick landscape; the scared serpent waits for them with his head high and his tongue forked. They give death.

They improvise stretchers. The sick men are no longer speaking. They are pale. The workers begin moving as quickly as possible to reach the camp. A deep and low moan that is emitted from those affected is heard. They are bleeding through their nose, mouth, and pores. The companions, when seeing the condition that they are in, start in a trot. They need to save their friends and brothers.

Now, the men bitten by the serpent begin to have seizures. They have dilated eyes. It is little they can do; the damn venom is doing its effect. They wonder how they can help them. How do they stop the poison? One of the sick men whispers that he doesn't want to die. He calls his mother, "Mama, I don't want to die!" All are frightened and confused because in their minds, they have formed the idea that they could have been bitten by the snake. They feel anger, pain, and ineptness. Under this chaos, they continue almost running through the difficult trails and marshes. They are submerged in an immense darkness. They are now certain that they will die; they think that the railway line will devour them.

Exhausted, they rest and cry. Through the fatigue, they take refuge in thinking about their families. Gregory moans in anguish of imagining if he were to lose his life, "Yemayá, what would become of my David? What would become my Edna and of my Pamela? I do not even think about it!" All take refuge in the memory of their families to escape the pain and death.

The terrible thing is that they are just beginning to face the dangers. They move on. They have aching muscles and numb toes. John Karruco approaches one of the sick men, who has his mouth open; the fat in his body has disappeared. Karruco tries to escape the pain and terror, but he can't do anything. They continue the march and listen to the weak moans. Syne has an obligation to stop the fear, and he gives his friends encouragement; however, his black eyes are reddening, his lips are trembling, and he starts to cry. Feeling his tears, he stops. He dries his face and continues the march.

It seems like a dream to everyone. They can't do anything for the sick. They cannot prevent them from suffering. They begin to understand that it is impossible to continue to go back. They notice jaw movement in the sick. Their faces are trembling somewhat. Their skin is purple; they no longer have the strength to fight against the venom.

The laborers who are transporting the stretchers stop, and they tearfully meditate; they realize that it is not worth persisting. Syne and Spencer whisper a prayer and wonder why life has to be painful for the poor. They lower their eyes to understand. The tears gush from everyone because of sadness.

They place those who are dying under some trees. They have blood-soaked clothes. The situation is dramatic. They have no other choice, and there is no medicine on hand that can save them; they seem powerless. Supported by the tree trunks, they observe how agonizingly slowly their friends are dying; and the only consolation is to be next to the dying. Gregory, with the feeling of emptiness, conceals his movements. He closes his eyes. Along with his companions, he digs a mass grave and buries the unfortunate men.

They breathe fresh air in order not to pass out. Karruco, with a husky voice, says a funeral prayer for the resting place of the workers killed on the job.

Everyone lifts their arms. They feel the need to force air back into their lungs. With pieces of branches, they make crosses that they place over the grave. They embark on the arduous road to the camp. But before they arrive, they encounter another crew that is searching the waters for three colleagues who have fallen in the mighty Pazán River, four kilometers to the north of Huigra—it was as if the wind had carried them. They tracked the waters up to the kilometers below but with no result.

The same Harman and Engineer Davis cry over the loss of their workers and constantly encourage them so that others do not get discouraged in their intention to see the railroad finished. They recognize the courage and devotion. They revive them, and the multitude of laborers listens in silence.

The events are left behind, in the past, by the surprising fact of having advanced some kilometers on the track. They place sleeping cots in the stillness of the silent and deserted mountain. Mister Harman daily telegraphs don Eloy; he communicates to him the multiple developments and informs him of the advances.

What is surprising is the tireless activity of the enlisted men and the perseverance with which they pursue the completion of the work. Barefoot and badly dressed, the laborers walk round, carrying and bringing materials; and they smile upon seeing their progress.

By the evening, they talk although, at times, their eyes fill to the brim with scenes of death; and under the light of the lightning, they unite their voices in chorus to say:

> *United Africa, because*
> *We are moving out of Babylon and*
> *We are going to the land*
> *Of our parents.*

On weekends, Karruco prepares the famous Jamaican chicken. In a campfire, he cooks a chicken and adds pineapple juice, a little coffee, and—when taking it out—he puts cheese in it.

Gregory is an expert in preparing *the quimbobó* with cornmeal;[6] he adds fish, with a preference of yam with coconut juice.

---

[6]   Quimbo[m]bó—refers to okra as well as a dish known as okra stew.

The laborers, eager for rest and fun, savor the typical food from their homeland, sing, banter, and play the guitar and drum in the light of the moon.

Michael Sandiford trusts that his god, who has broad powers, will protect him and will help him not to betray Jenny; however, he walks with anxious, demanding eyes like a beggar when he is with Luisa. He realizes that something is not going well; he doesn't know how or when or why Doña Miche's daughter has been tucked away in his thinking. He fights like a giant not to forget Jenny, but Luisa is taking a walk in a transparent nightie with a lantern in her hand; she is always forgetting something, searching and searching. He doesn't know what it is, but he acts as if he has not seen her. Suddenly, he hears Luisa's voice. "Michael, help me, please. I can't reach this jar."

"I'm going to face her, but I'll close my eyes so as not to look at her legs and beautiful rear that the nightie outlines. I open my eyes and see her solid body. Her silhouette is projected in the half-light, her voice rings out, and her words escape like a bird," he thinks. Her words are like the miracle of the loaves, and Michael is a paper boat that carries a cargo of stars. He is defenseless, without breathing, without touching anything so that his body does not betray him or produce any sounds that she can hear. Luisa moves from one side to another to find "I don't know what." She arranges and dishevels things, and Michael does not have anyone to ask for help or any place to take shelter. He would have to find a safe haven and as quickly as possible in order not to abandon his Jenny. He is afraid, he becomes quiet, and he does not want to harm his *Luna Llena* or his Luisa.

But Luisa stretches out in the grass, in a full moon. And her face seems like a blossoming rain; her lips, a panel of sweetness. "Michael, come, please. Scratch my back." His legs tremble, his voice shakes, and his fingers tremble; but he believes that God, with His generous hand, will continue to protect him. Luisa's voice is heard again; and she looks at Michael as he repeats her name with an expression of urgency, as if he were choking.

He does not know the origin of his tears when he shuns that body that is embracing him and those fingers that caress his entire body, and he's thinking of Jenny. He closes his eyes in order not to see Luisa's eyes that sprout from her blouse, and she exhales a scent of violet that sticks to his own. Michael feels something terrible, something which envelopes him. "No, my God, I have to return to Jamaica. How do I get out of this? And she—poor thing, you are alone in this jungle, without anyone to comfort you . . . I will not have pity, if she comes from a far country." The light superimposes Jenny's face onto Luisa's. Michael is afraid. It is that he will always remember his wife.

But he wonders if he will be able to support the desire that he has of going to bed with Luisa. "This woman has me crazy!" Although no other link exists other than the commitment of the skin, the pleasure of smells, and the mutual rubbing. It is wonderful. Both of them are intact; they are still safe.

Despite the intense fatigue and sadness, they experience moments of satisfaction knowing that they are working and that they are raising railway stations that will banish the darkness, and make it so that the coastal Ecuadorians may get to know the beauty of the Andes. They marvel at themselves about the valor and about confronting and withstanding the tests that they suffer.

Leona Cuebute's problem is maintaining her appearance as a man; to defend her job, she must continue with her disguise, which generates in her a deep feeling of anguish. She is willing to leave the camp when they offer her another job. Syne, who has finally discovered the secret, yearns for her; and he is full of silence thinking about her.

One morning, Engineer Henry Davis, who is part of The Guayaquil and Quito Railway Company, verifies that the grounds that the railway line is following are atrocious and are not providing safety to the railroad due to torrential rains, which have produced a severe landslide and have destroyed what is constructed.

The technicians show him the damage suffered. Harman, his face pale, overwhelmed and sad, decides to go to where the President of the Republic is to report the matter. "President, everything is lost. We are in the ruins!" The Old Warrior, dedicated to the necessity of maintaining his purpose, tries to keep the optimism and says, "First, don

Archer, let's take a drink of whisky to ward off the devil. Then we will see what to do."

Don Eloy clings tenaciously to the success; he increases efforts to find support in Congress, and he tries to calm the political opposition, which considers the construction of the railway a waste of money.

Of all the citizens, the only one who maintains a good spirit and who is marveled by the project is don Eloy, who works hard while his opponents continue to get the National Congress to deny a basis for the work.

The desire to escape from the routine, the weariness, the misfortunes, the hard work, and the tension required by the construction of the railway line, and to return tranquility to the spirit make Hugh Spencer and his companions build a soccer field. They clear a large space where there is only grass and croaking of frogs. With total activity and commotion, they use imagination, strength, and patience until they see the field finished.

Some of his friends do not know, nor do they have any idea what it is; but Hugh, ever-smiling, ensures that no detail is missing.

"Hey, explain what the game consists of."

"It provides agility and talent."

They affectionately pay attention; they are excited and in distress. He has managed to make a ball with pieces of leather; and with a strange and hoarse voice, he excites the interest and the passion for football.

"But what does it consist of? Talk fast!" They shout at him.

Everyone is silent. It is played on a rectangular field between two teams. At both ends of the ground are the goals, made by the space enclosed between two standing poles. The team that manages to get the ball more times in the arc of the opponent wins. And it is played with the feet.

"Then the question is to run and put the ball in the opposite goal."

"Yes!" They shout in chorus.

Once they understand, they rush into the game. Everything is ready. Hugh is happy; some are sporting green T-shirts and others, blue. But they have not fully understood the rules of the game. They form piles, they get emotional, they scream, they raise their hands and laugh, and they all forget the problems; they ease the sadness and the loneliness.

In Huigra, the laborers congregate around bonfires. All are seen with their faces in their hands, pensive. Engineer Henry Davis has red eyes from crying; he's thinking about the mountain, about the slippery terrain, about the rains that have complicated their projects and threatens to give a distinct destiny to the railway. So much money has been lost! And to think that the coffers are almost empty.

But he reacts and immediately seeks a safer way for the railway line. He needs to meditate and to draw up plans over and over again. In his spare time, in front of the campfire, or by early morning, he looks for the solution.

He withdraws from the gathering, worried about the mountain. He thinks that it can collapse again, and he superstitiously looks at it. At that moment, he begins to draw up a new sketch, a new route for the railroad, one that does not have a slope of more than three or four degrees. He now sees how all of those masses of land covered with trees are threatening, and he even sees the collapse in dreams. He trembles, believing that he hears the screams of terror of imprisoned laborers on being buried alive. He imagines the horrific, convulsive, and desperate moments that will be lived if the mountain collapses again while the men are working. That's why he keeps a watchful eye.

While they are sleeping, the torrential rain that dampens the materials—iron, sleeping cots, stone—is heard; everything is next to the road. It is early in the morning when a roar is heard, and they have the incredible impression that everything is collapsing. That formless mass of earth and trees slides back onto the railway line and into the river.

The group of laborers can't believe what they are seeing. It is the devil who does not want the railway constructed, and the comments generate questions and answers and more questions. The mountain has collapsed. It has plummeted on the materials; there is nothing to save or do. Everyone thinks that don Eloy will complicate their situation because of the great revolt that his enemies will assemble. They think that the great dream of the President will end badly. Opinions of that type are heard everywhere. They prefer to recount in detail the misfortune and wonder what they do now; it is likely that they will have to return to Jamaica.

But don Eloy knows the railroad will reach its destination; he remains firm in his purpose although the mountains may tumble. When thinking about it, his heart beats faster. His family supports him; his Anitilla gives him breath. That passion, his love for the homeland, and his faith in progress keep him optimistic. His family considers it admirable that this husband, father, brother, uncle dedicates his ability and talent to the well-being of the country. And to achieve this, he constructs the railroad.

The President immediately receives a clear and detailed report of the new route that the train will follow. And in a penetrating analysis of the causes of landslides, he agrees with Davis and Harman on the need to find a new, less dangerous route. Tormented by the setbacks, Harman, resisting beyond human patience, listens to the criticism of the political enemies of don Eloy ; he only thinks about how to help him as he increasingly admires him for his honesty and for his light-filled spirit, and he decides to leave in search of funding for the railway.

He travels to England, and as a businessman at the London Stock Exchange, he gets Ecuadorian bonds changed. The firm of Rubert Lubbeck and Company acquires a part in cash and, the other, through an issue of Condor Bonds—Ecuadorian gold coins equivalent to the pound sterling.

With the illusion that Alfaro has and Harman shares of the railroad climbing through the Andes, he experiences an immense happiness with the idea of getting the money. The fact is that his heart loves Ecuador with veneration.

One day, while walking along a London avenue, Mr. Harman approaches the Cathedral to pray and ask God for help with the most important work of Ecuador. After leaving the temple, he feels lively and looks for Mister James Sire Wright, multimillionaire philanthropist who collaborates with any promising company. Harman explains the project to him—the constant action of President Alfaro on solving the problem of poverty and his struggle of redistributing wealth so that the poor may have access to education and employment. Harman describes the landscape without forgetting the smell of the poplar trees, the song that emerges from the lips of the indigenous, the poncho woven with the colors of the rainbow, and many times one pure tear rolls down his cheek. Mister Harman recalls the condor, which soars to reach the stars. He affirms that the investment would be secured. He ends confirming to him: "For the rest of your life, you, Mister Wright, will be proud to have been associated with the great work of Ecuador's railway. Your contribution and momentum will be decisive."

The courageous words and the friendly way in which Harman describes the project make the philanthropist decide the future of the railway. When Archer hears his "magnificent," he sees the revival of Ecuador's railway, a kind of flourishing. It seems like a dream; it turns him toward the idea of triumph. He is sure that Wright has a generous heart and a great talent.

He does not question the conditions since between high-minded people, they do not need to sign documents. The word has moral force, and this only justifies that Mister James Sire Wright becomes shareholder of what is called The Guayaquil and Quito Railway Company.

Meanwhile, in Ecuador, the opposition is strongly organized to raise a protest against Alfaro and Harman. The enemies assert that the railway is a fantasy or delirium of the elder Alfaro because catastrophe is in sight. They are saying that the President of the Republic and Harman created fraudulent businesses. Conservatives hate them because they are both Protestants.

Don Eloy never tires of saying that the train will be the best teacher; it is part of his life, of his work, and of his activities. And his most important concern is to get the money, which he completely lacks. Another concern of Alfaro is the desperate task of turning off pockets of resistance that are increasingly more passionate; however, he persists optimistically with strength and good spirits in respect to the train project. For this reason, when Harman tells him the news of the financing success, he cries for joy.

They work until the sun sets. Lamboreo, always talkative (his soul is still Jamaican), very happily laughs on imitating his peers. His friends come together with him to spend pleasant moments. This young boy—who with his jokes makes them forget their sorrows, concerns, and worries—plays the drum next to John Karruco, who has taught him to move his fingers with mastery. He tells a series of memories and anecdotes, and he makes the hours pass more calmly and bearably. All laugh at his quips and he receives applauses.

The next day, the President of the Republic appears dressed with his *jipijapa* hat and a poncho. He comes to observe the severity of the mudslides and finds the laborers working with picks and shovels to remove mud and earth. He is living in the flesh the tragedies of the workers, the major players of the railroad who open the jungle where they find a sign of a road. Don Eloy hears the rattling of the iron, like a song sung by the railway line. He enthusiastically congratulates Henry Davis and Morley.

His visits become more frequent in order to give confidence and encouragement to the enlisted men; he understands how difficult that work is under such a strong sun, and in winter weather, the rain is torrential. Like a father, he encourages the laborers that if there should exist some disagreement among them, dialoging is better to make the task more reasonable and worthy. He doesn't forget to recommend to them to have faith in God.

For the laborers, don Eloy is the image of goodness and tenderness. With the simplicity that characterizes him, he asks Leona for a little water. "Son, give me a glass of water."

The Jamaican disguised as a man runs and brings a crystal glass with a liquid so clear and cold that don Eloy asks her about its origin. Leona tells him that it is from the waterfall. He smiles.

In Bucay, the crews are organized under the direction of Engineer Davis. The situation has returned to normal, and the work progresses. He feels satisfaction about the effectiveness of the workers.

The vast distances and difficult situations prevent smooth communication, and he uses the *churo*[7] to communicate with the crews.

---

[7] Churo—it is a shell shape, coiled wind instrument found in the Andes

They leave behind a few camps and others rise. Bridges are built to overcome obstacles and to fight the threat of flooding rivers. He has organized a body of expert workers in reading the new plans outlined by Davis. (It is the route that continues parallel to the Garcia Moreno thoroughfare, the safest line.) Bridges of lime and stone are built along the railway line as solid resistance.

Technicians are now very confident in the stability of the ground because the respective analysis of soil has been made.

Work is done around the clock, trees keep on knocking down under the contumacious rain, which when it clears is called "little winter"; then, the temperature fluctuates between 25 and 27 degrees centigrade while in the "big winter" the temperature climbs to 34 degrees. And it is then when the rivers drag trees, animals, and ranches until drowned; and the insects fly scared in gigantic swarms.

The contractors' action is to give strength and to encourage the laborers who can't even talk without the bugs getting into their mouths. All are worried about those red mosquitoes called gnats that cause irritating bites.

The camps wait for the twentieth of each month so that Economist Eduardo Morley can pay their wages; then the celebration comes, and in the evening, they meet at doña Miche Cuello's (whom they nickname *la Pava*) or in the Nicholas Montalvo canteen (alias *el Futre*). And to stop being killed by malaria, they drink *chilicay* liquor. Together—gringos, Ecuadorians, and Jamaicans—in a sympathetic attitude and in the spirit of collaboration, discuss the hardships and the suffering. With liquor love and romance. Tempers bloom.

There is a round in which each one recalls something of his life, his country, his desires, and his fears. There in the cantina and away from their families, Jamaicans listen to the thunder that defies the rays, they speak, speak, words, words in that insane dream to return to their country with money. John Karruco plays the drum. All look at the hands that make tunes spring from the instrument that he has inside: soft, billowing, filled with sorrows and joys, half resignation, half hope. His fingers are touching memories. They are faces, abundant faces, and lots of people talking to relieve their tensions. Gregory cries while remembering David, Pamela, and Edna; so far he has not hit on the promised gold. Michael cries for his Jenny. Mister Davis, already with his glasses of liquor from chilicay inside his chest, also talks about his passions, his joys, and his faith in his future life although almost no one understands him because he is speaking in English and is even crying in that language. He is simply a human being who also feels infinite nostalgia.

The American, the Jamaicans, and the natives all leave embracing, singing in chorus; they have also drunk because of the success of the railroad.

She drops down on the grass. Luisa is wearing a red silk skirt and a black linen blouse. Michael Sandiford follows her. She lifts her eyes to look at him, and it seems impossible to him that a single girl is so beautiful. He thinks that if she were to meet Jenny, both would seem like one sun.

He stretches out on the grass, and Luisa embraces him with the same emotion as Jenny. She has her same smell, her same touch; and when kissing her, he feels exactly the same. Both have the magic formula to transform him into a bonfire.

While Luisa takes a step toward Michael, Jenny withdraws and becomes non-existent under the transparent skirt that Luisa is wearing; and gradually, the recollection of that other skin is removed from Michael's memory.

On Monday morning, the laborers are en route to carry out their tasks. The breeze refreshes. Lamboreo notices chills, headache, and exhaustion; however, he hopes that the discomfort passes. Many thoughts are crossing his mind: he wonders if it is that malignant fever that is killing the laborers. It occurs to him to chew the tender stems of plants that are within his reach, and he feels some relief.

They keep on working—either with a machete, a pick, or a shovel. At noon, when the sun is at its full splendor, Lamboreo trembles from cold; and he falls to the ground. Leona, who is always by his side, screams frightened when she sees him pale and trembling. She applies a dressing of mud on his stomach. She quickly grinds very green leaves, mixes them with lemon, and gives them to him to drink. At the beginning, the sick man refuses to take the bitter and unpleasant taste; but Leona forces him, and Lamboreo must accept the remedy.

They must return to camp. Syne, Spencer, and Taylor accompany the patient, who lets go of Leona's arm. They impatiently move forward since the fever is getting worse, and Lamboreo almost can't walk, forcing his colleagues to carry him.

Arriving at the meeting, they find Engineer Davis trembling from fevers and with an intense headache. He is transported to the special camp of the gringos; his condition is delicate since he has no safeguards to combat the disease.

There is a great silence in the camp, meetings are halted, and the population is aware of their health status. Lamboreo continues ingesting the remedies given to him by his friend (after all, he loses nothing by accepting them); and between his teeth, he is heard to say "Leona, don't kill me." And she replies, "What else can I do if the pills run out?" Desperate, she grinds herbs, removes the juice, and gives the drink to the sick man; and with it, she manages to get the fever down.

The medicines brought from the United States do not have the effect on Engineer Davis; his condition is serious, and the doctor makes a great effort to save his life and, with it, the work of the railway. He made the design of the route safer, avoiding the danger that encloses the River Chanchán.

Without a doubt, the foreign remedies do not work to combat tropical diseases that have been in the camps. The infected complain of severe headaches and of aching bones, and they suffer from high temperatures that finally produce death. Lamboreo's fever has gone up; he knows that he is going to die, and his great dream of returning to his country with money will have been only that: a dream. The railway, to his knowledge, is a dragon that swallows the laborers, a kind of combat which not even the animals or vegetation will save. His fever has risen higher. He is delirious and he imagines birds flying scared, crazed, trying to save themselves from the train; but in the jungle, the trees, with such beauty, are being torn down to build the sleeping cots with them. He will not live long. In his agony, he hears the bells of the only temple they built. Meanwhile, Leona is constantly applying compresses and gives him the concoction to drink with lemon juice.

The doctor stops in front of the platforms. He thinks about all the faces and discovers that the sick have the same symptoms and that every day the number of infected increases. The teenager hopes to be examined by the doctor—who walks slowly, pensive, his face dropped in sadness. Nobody escapes from the same diagnosis, and he finds that it is essential to look for help.

He widens the organization to prevent infection, but there are no sanitary conditions in the camps; they don't even have ventilation. He thinks that he is playing with death; his efforts to save his patients are in vain. He is committed to preventing the cause of the disease, to investigating its source, and to applying his findings to save lives. He begins to discuss the issue and to look for answers. He fears mistakes. His biggest interest is to identify the insect that causes the fever. Now it's the question of the survival of the laborers.

He thinks about Engineer Davis for a long time. The Doctor's state of health is very delicate. He is aware that his life is in danger. He cannot stop the epidemic; he has lost, and his face has turned yellow. He sees tears slipping down his cheeks. For several days, he has been between life and death; his heart beats morosely.

For the doctor, this is a torture that produces helplessness; he feels unable to stop the disease. He regrets that his skills are not sufficient to prevent death. *Who is to blame? Who is torturing and killing?* Those are the reflections that distress him.

Davis no longer belongs to the world of the living. It is already too late to save him, and it is also too late to live because he can be left with serious injury in the brain. The doctor takes his head with both of his hands and cries.

In the other camps, the story is repeated exactly the same way. Last night it rained; and the water, upon seeping through the door, has transformed the earth of the floor into mud. The air inside the camps feels heavy and is loaded with carbon dioxide. Lamboreo opens his eyes. He doesn't know how long he has been ill. He knows nothing about what is happening. He has not even seen the sunlight. Lying on the pallet, he hears complaints from the sick men. He doesn't even remember how he got there or who brought him. He has to stay still for hours. His back and bones hurt. He does not remember where he is: he remembers absolutely nothing. It occurs to him for the first time that those suffering men most closely resemble ghosts that emerged suddenly from another world with their cadaveric faces. He looks at them and he is scared; he wonders if he is in the cemetery. He believes that death is an immediate threat and that he will not escape it.

A psychological struggle begins, which agitates the adolescent. The work of the railway turns into a tragedy, but nevertheless, the workers do not limit their effort in the slightest; the ultimate conviction to see the railway climbing the Andes remains latent. They are prepared to make the project a reality. They are committed to winning, striving to move forward in the Andes mountain range that extends its majesty and its steep power.

The adolescent closes his eyes, and he touches his forehead. He does not have a fever, but he feels very weak. He lets time pass. His tongue passes along his gums to avoid the anguish of feeling a dry mouth and throat. He recalls that Leona has left him a lemon, and he sucks on it. Later he hears voices and footsteps, but he doesn't care who they may be. His weakness does not allow him to have an interest. He returns to his semiconscious state. He notices that his strength has abandoned him; he wants to get up but he can't. He strains to cling to the edge of the scaffold, and upon taking a step, he collapses. He is sure that soon they will take him to the platform to carry him to the mass grave.

He manages to sleep on the pallet. He is sure that the laborers selected to drag off the dead will soon come for him. He moves aside the thought of that idea. He doesn't even look at the doorway of the hut for fear of being buried alive.

He has never felt as afraid as at this moment. He closes his eyes and falls asleep. But he is suddenly aware that someone is pushing him. He falls to the ground, and they drag him by his legs. Light seems to heavily penetrate his eyelids, burning the temples like an ember.

He hears shouting, and a woman throws herself on him to hug him; but she is violently separated. Every day similar scenes are seen.

Leona is the one in despair for her friend, and she throws herself on Lamboreo's body to avoid him being taken to the platform.

The situation remains serious in the camps; the plague causes a great loss of lives, which hinders the normal progress of the work. The doctor has ordered them to cut the grass in the vicinity of the enclosed fields and then burn it in order to kill the insects; however, the presence of mosquitoes is permanent.

The men who are dragging Lamboreo struggle with Leona. Some minutes pass, and finally her friend moves his arms and opens his eyes to listen to the cries he cannot identify. He strains to leave the world of the unconscious, where he has been submerged for days. Leona studies the sick man's face. Now she is sure that he is not dead. She forgets about the contagion and runs to stop the man who is dragging Lamboreo toward the platform that is full of corpses. She shouts out loud, "He's alive! He's alive!" The man stops. Every day they take platforms full of corpses to a cemetery raised along the Angas River at kilometer 106.

Lamboreo's voice trembles; the terror of being buried alive almost kills him. Leona goes back to talk to him, and she caresses his forehead, still feeling the fear of losing her friend. She lifts him by placing her arms under his armpits. She does it with ease: the patient weighs as little as a child. He no longer has a fever although the dizziness persists. His colleagues are amazed; the teenager has survived the crisis.

The doctor examines him. He tries to understand what has saved him. He is sure that because he is young and has high defenses, he was able to overcome the effects of the disease. Lamboreo's large eyes cry from gratitude. For many, it is a miracle of Yemayá.

The sacrifices have not finished because they have not yet concluded the work. The laborers were unaware, before leaving their country, of the difficult conditions in which the tasks would be developed. The temple bells ring at night. They strike and strike with despair. Those who live in the camp believe that something serious is happening.

Initially they remain quiet, and then they run to see what is happening. The main authority is going to break the news. Without hiding the sadness, he makes an effort not to cry.

Usually workers demonstrate sensitivity to those who die; however, it is the first time they hear an alarm playing. Nobody knows what has happened, but they suspect that something very serious is happening. They are impatient to hear the news. Some suspect that President Eloy Alfaro was overthrown by a revolt of the conservatives or that he has died. *What has happened?*

The night is darker than ever. The laborers form large groups, and something similar to fear reflects in their faces. The informant swallows saliva. He dries the tears; and with a trembling voice, he says, "Engineer Henry Davis has died."

They cannot contain the crying. At that moment, they understand the terrible news; and they know that the railway project is in danger. No one knows who is responsible for the evil that is decimating the workers. *Who is to blame? Is it a spirit that comes from the river?* They have the feeling of being sentenced and that sooner or later fate will come for them. Night envelops them in a dense and sad darkness.

The death of Engineer Henry Davis produces a deep vacuum. For the first time, Herman feels without strength; and very sadly, he communicates to President Alfaro—who, dismayed, informs his ministers. And the sorrow is very deeply felt throughout the country. The confusion is clear, and publicly they recognize the sacrifice and delivery of Davis and so many others who have fallen in the service of the country.

In the camps, the spirit of Engineer Davis' work gives them strength to move forward. The bonfire lights the faces of laborers who like to go there to sing, to discuss or recall stories and customs from their places of origin. They mix the melodies of their grandparents with romantic songs, influenced by the loneliness and the brandy that they drink to kill the nostalgia. That light blinks, and often wind devours the embers and extinguishes them; but in the darkness, the gathering continues.

The time they have remaining in the camps has influence on the workers, and the campfire becomes witness to their feelings of sadness and happiness. The nostalgia is so deep at night that the moon inspires memories; and all sing noisily while John Karruco plays the drum and others, the guitar. Syne looks at the moon. He thinks about Leona, young, vital, and playful.

One morning while don Eloy stops to review the work, he looks tired. The fight against landowners in favor of the poor who do not pay taxes is hard because they arm uprisings in the *sierra*. But he remains determined to organize a social change.

Sometimes it is difficult to fall asleep as many problems remove his tranquility. On that occasion while sharing with the workers, he meets Lamboreo and is surprise that as a teenager, he is working on the railway line. He stops in front of the boy who, scared, battered in his clothes, and with eyes that still reflect his having been sick, does not know what to say.

He does not know what don Eloy wants and nervously greets him. "Do you want to come with me to my house? You're very young to work." It seems like a dream—strange and unreal—as if he were offering him paradise.

"What's your name?"

"Aniceto Lamboreo," he stutters, lowering his gaze and trembling with emotion. He fails to understand what is happening.

The teenager moves his head affirmatively. "Yes, yes." The President looks at the bewildered young man as he walks beside him.

From that day on, Leona feels hopeless and contemplates leaving the camp; she feels seized by vertigo in Lamboreo's absence. Memory becomes a flood, and the moon is the recipient of her sorrows. She daily exhales tears since Lamboreo has said goodbye, leaving her a bunch of promises. His new family has become don Eloy, and he will have the considerations and the goodness that characterize the Alfaros; however, she knows that he will always remember his life in the camp.

The absence of the young man influences Leona to think seriously about changing jobs. She considers Ventura Villavicencio's proposal, who lives in Quito and who will pay a good salary and who will give her food and housing. But she does want to see the railway line completed.

For a long time, the laborers have known that Leona is a daring girl who posed as a man; but her disguise did not always hide her, and she is teased for her fictitious identity.

One morning she dresses herself in her colorful skirt and attractive turban. Now the looks toward Leona increase; young men surround her and she laughs. She knows how to get out of the moment. She hopes that don Eloy will take her to work in his home.

Her friendship with the Marret brothers and John Karruco serve as comfort and protection. One clear night, in front of the fire, Syne is ready to declare his love. He feels very attracted by the strength he notices in Leona, by the determination with which she has regained her life. Now she is not afraid of being fired from the job for being a woman, and she wears skirts in bright and strong colors that accentuate her feminine grace.

With Syne, they talk about music, dances, myths, and the characters of his town. The atmosphere is different from the feverish daily tasks: the laughter and the jokes are not expected. They miss Lamboreo, who with his imitations made these get-togethers fun.

The conversation unfolds without being aware of the humid heat or the cold in the morning that surrounds the camp. The rains make the air sticky and grey; however, the laborers are still without anyone noticing the time. Syne calms the emotions that he is living. He aims to convince Leona not to leave the camp, but he feels afraid to express the anguish of losing her. He longs for her to realize that he loves her. Leona Cuebute, distracted, looks around her; she believes that her love should have the scent of poplar trees, of the orchids that are born in the jungle. She lifts her head, meditates, and thinks of her mother. *What is she doing?* She is beginning to live for herself, and listening with pride to the praise and compliments of her companions, she smiles aware of her friends' glances of admiration. She likes Syne Marret, but he does not decide to declare his love for her.

In the jungle lights, they gradually build railway stations, lights that give life to the laborers. They battle with the abysses, they battle against the sun and rain, they bury the shadows, and they cross torrential rivers; and the landscapes are chiseling dreams. Men and women are shouting as they offer their products. Horses are neighing. The crawlers and flutes are waking up the eyes of the angels. An unprecedented vision, a parade of vendors, defy the silence.

Now, a sonorous flurry develops at each station that opens. A real exhilaration is observed; new work sources have been discovered. And every Sunday, the women take advantage to show their traditional costumes; and they add beauty to the scenery.

Bucay is famous for its "steel water" brandy, which consists of introducing a steel rod that pushes the firewood for the operation of the railway into the brandy.

They call Huigra "the station of eternal spring." Here, its inhabitants sell cooked egg in a cabbage leaf, corn, and pork rinds. At this station, a Chinese citizen with the last name Chail sets up his business; and there Leona learns to prepare Chinese food. She also observes how industrious his family is and their spirit of savings.

The young woman is impressed to learn that all diseases can be cured with different kinds of tea; and every day, for a few minutes, she is paralyzed when faced with the rites carried out by the family when it comes to tea.

She does not understand the why of consuming so much of that drink although they say it has an exquisite fragrance and country aroma that invites you to drink it. For her the tea is bitter, and it does not pass down her throat; then she focuses on moistening her lips, then, takes small sips in order to finish savoring the cup.

She reflects on the Chail family and their habit of eating rice without salt or oil. They eat with ivory chopsticks. They move them with great ease as if they were tableware. The family's manner of greeting also calls her attention; the members incline their body and join hands together. They never change character because no one ever hears them shouting or raising their voice. They are not angry, and they are always willing to talk about their country.

A real problem for Leona is understanding what Chail is talking about; however, her interest in recipes and how to prepare the tea facilitates her learning. She needs to know how to cook all of the recipes because she wants to leave the camp although she is in love with Syne.

One night, the laborers are astonished that Leona is speaking to them about the Shang dynasty, the Chin dynasty, and who built the Great Wall. For the first time, the Jamaicans have the opportunity to listen to her talk about these things.

The young woman's thought above all is that she cannot last beyond her departure. She will lose some of the happiness that her friends give her, but her fate is sealed. She knows that she runs the risk of living without the protection of her friends, but she has to become the protagonist of her future; she may have the possibility of obtaining better things. One afternoon, while her peers are away from camp, she leaves with the cloak she signed on with. It is a cloak with figures of flowers and seaweed. She stops a moment. Her attitude suggests that the pain of leaving is enormous; she carries in her heart torn photographs of Syne, Gregory, John, Spencer, Sandiford, Mackenzie, and Taylor. She leaves to work as a domestic in the home of Ventura Villavicencio, in Quito.

Months later Luisa goes shopping at the Eterna Primavera Department Store—which is owned by the Zurita family, for whom some Jamaicans who decided to settle in Huigra work. So they have given another direction to their lives, and they sigh for a better future.

The cities, parishes, precincts, as well as a shuffling of customs, religions, and nationalities are all getting entangled. The Ecuadorians, Peruvians, Chinese, Jamaicans, Colombians, and Italians will be the ships that come and go every moment.

Peace and joy fill Luisa's heart; she now possesses an internal sun, and she is pregnant. She wants a girl because according to the midwife, it will be a girl. When Luisa climbs the bleachers, she raises her left foot first, which corresponds to the heart and which explains why women love more than men.

Now, she is going to buy clothes for her daughter. She will acquire pink for her to follow the tradition and prevent a tomboy, and when she comes out . . . "When I give birth . . . so much is missing. My God, how much is missing! I cannot walk with this belly. Four more months, weeks, days, days, days . . . It will be a Sunday—Wednesday. That day my little girl will be born! I do not want it to be Sunday because that is a day Michael puts himself in a trance as if he were heading up a funeral procession, and one sees him drying his tears with the handkerchief." That's why Luisa does not want the girl to be born on Sunday since her husband dresses up in his Sunday's best in such a way that he becomes unbearable, and gradually, he is populating distant places where he sees remote landscapes.

Sometimes, she feels that Michael embraces her and immerses in her breasts to look there for the thin body of Jenny, that black and shiny skin; then, she is afraid that her husband may leave and return to Kingston. Of course, there is that possibility. How can she deny it? "Where is Jenny? How can I know if Michael is enclosed in his hermeticism, in what she herself does not know?"

One night Luisa applies almond oil on her enormous belly, on her buttocks, and on her breasts to prevent stretch marks. "God free me!"

She knows that Michael is like the others—his fellow Jamaicans—and he will never be hers; however, she invents things, invents passion. It is also possible to be happy in this way.

One afternoon, Luisa sees her husband coming with a box. Now she walks slowly.

"I cannot walk anymore with this belly. It seems that they are twins."

He kisses her on the mouth and says to her, "Guess what I have in this box . . ."

"What?"—She is pensive.—"Cookies . . ."

"No. Close your eyes. It is a gift for the woman that I love most, and I will love the rest of my life."

"For me?"

"No."

Luisa's voice stops. She opens her mouth. She needs air. She can't believe it. "My God! It is for Jenny. This man will return to Jamaica," her heart tells her.

"Open your eyes," he orders her.

She focuses her view and sees that Michael has a doll in his hands. She smiles and hugs her husband's body.

Until one Tuesday, almost a month later, Luisa gives birth to a girl. Michael caresses his wife's hand. For so long, he has wanted to be a father. The mother smiles. "Yes, he will stay with me," she thinks. They "*matatiruntirulan*[8] and this girl will be called Luisa Sandiford Valle." Michael puts his daughter to sleep.

They all rest at home. A ray of sunshine lights the garden, and Luisa experiences a deep sense of regret. Her husband breathes the fresh and light air. He seems to be waiting for someone as he is seated, looking in the distance. "It is Jenny. He cannot forget her. Michael will return to his country," she says to herself, drying the tears with her hands. Upon realizing the woman's presence, Michael runs to toss the ball in a hoop that he had improvised at the bottom of the garden.

There is don Eloy. He has aged. He is modestly dressed. He has a somewhat taciturn, pale face; but he is still actively at work. He takes enough time to observe the progress of the work of the last fortnight. He congratulates the technicians. A large part of the railway has already been built: ten stations corresponding to the province of Guayas and four to the Chimborazo.

He takes a step forward. He squeezes the cane and continues looking at the beauty of the landscape. He has friendly words for the trees, thanks them, and asks for forgiveness. He lifts his eyes to heaven, to the cosmic life, like someone who is nourished by light and observes the happiness caused by listening to the murmur of water and a flute that cries music.

He has come to say goodbye to the technicians and laborers, to congratulate them because they demonstrated their ability to overcome the difficulties and dangers for the construction of the railway line, and because of the vital importance for the development of the economy of Ecuador.

His words, according to the workers, are those of an idealist and a poet. He is a person of honor and a delicate spirit. They understand that he has not managed to continue with the gigantic work. His farewell turns into a demonstration of affection, in which hundreds of laborers lift their arms and shout, "Don Eloy, don Eloy, long live

---

[8]   matantiruntirulan is a play on words that is used in the rounds for children, almost always in the kindergarten (defined by Chiriboga)

Alfaro, Alfaro!" They support him for his vertical attitude and honesty and because they understand the political environment in which his government is developing. "Let Syne Marret talk!" they insist. They are silent. Syne waits a moment. He looks at his peers who signal for him to talk. He frowns. He has never spoken in public; worse still, in front of a person so illustrious. What madness they have asked of him! How does it happen that his friends ask that of him? He struggles to maintain his calm as he walks toward don Eloy.

"Don Eloy . . ."

He does not raise the tone of his voice, but he feels a compulsion that takes him by surprise.

"Don Alfaro, you have made a great effort to build this railway. Already, you cared about everyone's health, that everyone has work, that everyone got somethin' to eat, that they know how to read and write. You fight against the bad guys and the rich men who cheat. You is a good person, don't steal, and you is always with the one who don't have nothing."

"Bravo! Bravo! May Yemayá give to you health and also to your family. May Lamboreo continue with you and that his attitude is good."

"Bravo, bravo!"

It is the tribute that one pays to the Old Warrior. Don Eloy's eyes cloud over, and through his tears, he looks at the laborers; he understands that this is the most sincere recognition he has received.

He uses more than words of gratitude; in truth, he had not even thought that laborers were aware of the political situation in the country. He announces that he has finished his presidential term and that he is happy because the train has made progress through Duran, Milagro, Naranjito, Barraganetal, Bucal Naranjapata, and Huigra. At each station, he has seen how the faces of the people light up as new towns, customs, foods, and habits are born. The railway has changed the fate of their lives.

At each station, the name of Alfaro is a burning cry, like water that purifies. It has the fresh and joyful smell of fruit. Seeds on fertile soil. At each station, they follow his footprint; and with a vigilant ear, they cheer the revolutionaries. At each station is heard "Long live Alfaro, dammit."

He knows the next President of the Republic will continue the work because one hundred and fifty thousand *libras* are being held by the trustee, a deposit that gave extraordinary value to the railway bonds and morally served a great deal of the company business in broadening its credit. He will continue the route planned by Henry Davis; it has no possibility of error, and it is the safest.

He has named Commander in Chief of the Army of the Littoral to General Leonidas Plaza Gutiérrez (thirty-four years of age) in order to establish relations with the Liberals on the coast and to tighten the friendship with officials. General Plaza Gutiérrez has lived a great deal of time abroad, and for that same reason, he does not know the country.

When talking, a great optimism is reflected on Alfaro's face; and he is enthusiastic when he refers to his political peer because he knows of his qualities and his sincerity. His words climb the mountain range of the Andes; they cross the stormy rivers, and with the wind, they ride to remote regions where the sun rides plows of hope.

His nobility tries to demonstrate that his favorite candidate is General Leonidas Plaza Gutiérrez; he trusts him. It is indispensable to place in him the programs and projects of social and economic claim that he had undertaken.

He has visited all the camps converted into villages where building materials and elements of subsistence are abundant. The President's fingers touch one of Major Harman's shoulders. He does it with admiration and gratitude as if he were touching a brother or an Ecuadorian who had carried out an act of courage. The workers also consider him one of the promoters of the railway. He loves Ecuador, and for don Eloy, it is a true joy to have found a person with the virtues of Harman.

The laborers cannot contain their emotion and exclaim, "Long live Mister Harman!"

Major Harman, although he does not like speak a great deal, on this special occasion, he is encouraged to take the floor.

"I don't like to be conceited. However, my obligation is to acknowledge the qualities attributed to me by the President." His blue eyes are still watching don Eloy. Major Harman reflective mode and his discipline influence him to express his humility and gratitude.

"Long live Mister Harman!" He appreciates it by lifting one of his arms.

For Alfaro it is impossible to stop referring to this foreigner who comes with all his strength to devote himself to such a gigantic work as the Trans-Andean Railway. Harman appreciates it and smiles. As don Eloy continues with the praise, he blushes. "I am confident that you will continue to work with the next president."

They pass through the camp. Major Harman explains to don Eloy that they will continue opening the rails; and he confirms the plans plotted by Davis—always along the Kelly Highway and avoiding the fearsome Chanchan River.

Seeing the rails, the thoughts of both coincide although neither expresses them. They remember that up until that moment, the one who gives the orders is don Eloy; but then . . . The two look at the horizon, but optimism floats to the surface; and they have faith that God will bless the Trans-Andean Railway.

The next president must have the same purpose as don Eloy and not give credence to claims of his political opponents: that because of the train, atheism would arrive, a repeated argument of the conservatives.

They stop. Alfaro lifts his gaze to the sky as if asking for help. He has the air of someone who is accustomed to praying. He is happy because he is sure that Harman will monitor it, and he will continue to seek help for the work.

It is absurd, from the political point of view, that he should suspend construction if the expenses are perfectly justified. No one can accuse him of not leaving money to continue the work: the plans, locomotives, and engineers are ready.

After a few days, he will no longer be president. He closes his eyes in order not to see the thickness of the forest; perhaps he will never return to those sites again. When he opens his eyes, the sun is on his face and his sadness fades.

On the way back, Harman looks for more appropriate words to wish him good health in his private life and to say that working with him has taught him the ability to continue believing in mankind. Harman sighs sadly; his brother John is buried in that place.

Upon arriving at the camp, John Karruco has already prepared the Jamaican chicken, made with pineapple juice, a serving of coffee, and cheese. Gregory offers them *quimbobo*, and the inhabitants of Huigra have worked hard on fixing a table that glitters with corn, cheese, eggs, and pork rinds.

When sharing the meal, there is laughter. All are seated on pieces of wood that at times serve as benches. Don Eloy regains his appetite, and at the same time, he asks questions without stopping and chats in a very good mood. They realize Alfaro's simplicity; he is accustomed to sharing with peasants and humble people. Lamboreo notices that he is very tired; nevertheless, he is encouraged when he drinks a sip of steel water. The audience applauds. The workers stand with their voices in chorus and raise a prayer for don Eloy's well-being.

CHAPTER THREE

*T*he day started out dark with a gust of wind hitting the workers' faces. They silently move forward. Occasionally a group stops to protect themselves. Along the trail, the cold has left them with indelible marks.

The huge mountains block the way; some have human-like figures, and others resemble animals. Behind them, the camps stand out like a tiny speck. The Marret brothers lead the crew; and they look at the plan—which the new technician, Engineer Wio Bennett, gave them, with approval of the President Leonidas Plaza Gutiérrez.

Suddenly a huge snowfall vigorously hits. Snow falls silently all morning. The thick whiteness makes it difficult for them to advance, and they need to walk carefully because they run the risk of falling into the abyss.

Winding trails make the inspection dangerous. The rocks have a dark, moldy color because of time and silence. The laborers stop to count off and find out if any are missing. The same numbers are huddled together and receive the warmth of a friend; at these heights, they feel more like brothers. As they ascend, the dangers intensify.

On one side is the cliff; and on the other side, an inaccessible mountain that they will have to drill in order to make way for the railway line. They rub their hands, stretch their legs, and jump to avoid the numbness. Syne feels badly; altitude sickness is wreaking havoc on his lower limbs, and they have begun to freeze in that sea of white and gray. The stiffness of his feet concerns him. The laborers are looking for the exit before night falls. Syne's face is pale. He takes a look around. He wonders if he will die at these heights. He moves forward with a dry throat, and from time to time, he jumps to keep the circulation going.

Upon arriving at the camp, he is anxious to find Leona to express his love to her. Where could she be (and with whom)? He has no strength and faints when he enters the sleeping area. John Karruco, with the help of their friends, takes Syne to the pallet, where his skillful hands and his magical recipes relieve Syne. He gives him a massage with alcohol that has been heated up with some herbs and wrapped in a tiger's skin.

The healer is famous inside and outside of the camp for healing with massages and prayers, but he is also very well-known for the preparation of the typical dishes of his country. These skills serve him as a shelter and protect him from what he has lost. A form of anesthesia allows him to overcome any angst, and although he cannot deny his past, he is forced not to look back.

He occupies his hands, which he always keeps in motion; and he, thus, vents the contained emotions that agitate him inside. Syne and Gregory are the one ones who understand his heartache, and they empathize with him. John's father and two of his brothers are blind, and he had decided to help them out. He possesses the capacity and an unwavering faith to keep his family together.

The Marret brothers understand the reasons for his sadness, and they justify his preoccupation. In those circumstances, John cannot afford even to express his pain or his nostalgia; he knows that there is no time for tears, and he cannot fail—nor can he stop in the middle of the road. His conscience and the memory of his father and brothers will not allow it. He is living in a different world than that of Jamaica. He sometimes wonders the same thing as all of his companions: will he return alive? He feels the need to wrap himself in a greater strength in order to resist. It is a way to survive the new customs, beliefs, people, climate, and tastes. They all have really resisted. They have replaced one existence with another one. They have had to adapt in order to find a space in a new environment, and they have learned to love Ecuador.

This healer gives massages based on the oil of jungle animals. He skillfully twists and he puts bones in their place. His oily fingers move up and down to connect the bone that came out of its place. When he is not working on the railway line, he dedicates himself to investigating the benefits of plants. He is also an expert in the kitchen, and he prepares a tasty rice dish with coconut: he cooks a half pound of pigeon peas and rice, to which he adds half a liter of coconut juice. This dish has become famous among the Americans and the natives who savor it warmly. In this way, John Karruco controls his tormented silences so they will not transform into a crisis.

Two days later, the group reports to Engineer Bennett—who, knowing the dangers that the work entails, prepares to set the mood so that the workers will not be frightened. He has an interest in taking the railway to the summit called *La nariz del diablo* (The Devil's Nose), whose incline of five to six degrees is very dangerous. He adamantly opposes any suggestions of technicians or workers. It is in vain to discuss it; it is a waste of time. Day after day, week after week, he affirms that the change in the railway route is convenient. Perhaps the most terrible thing will be the human suffering, the enormous test of sorrow that the workers will face.

They are divided into crews: those who are located at kilometer 108 raise two steel bridges 35.7 meters and 36.3 meters of light, a distance of two blocks, above the Chanchán River. In addition, they form embankments that are parallel to the river, which causes terrible difficulties and drawbacks that delay the tasks.

Other crews are located between the kilometers 110 and 114, where a bridge has to be built in the form of an S, a very difficult task because death lurks at every step. Syne, Spencer, Sandiford, Mackenzie, and Taylor are familiar with the original plan designed by Engineer Davis. That is why they wonder what motives or what interests exist to alter the established trail; they believe that the change is a death sentence for the railway. Compared to this grim alternative, they foresee horrible sacrifices; they know that Morley's foolhardiness of wanting to reach the summit of the Andes will be a work that will cost a lot of blood.

They do not know the reasons why President Leonidas Plaza Gutiérrez and Morley have changed the original plans. *Why follow the riverbed of the mighty Chanchán River that sows terror in its path?*

At times, they remain motionless. They call out Engineer Davis' name and look at the stars lost in the sky. They already know that the route change has been made with Plaza's consent, who is allowing the construction to pass through the mountain peak with a slope of up to six percent; and on the other hand, the trail drawn by Davis was only three percent. They lament Harman's absence (he is out of the country seeking bonds).

He is also changing the fate of the Trans-Andean Railroad since Economist Morley is acquiring extensive lands where the railway line will pass through and will earn added capital. Ecuadorians and foreigners are forced to buy land from him to build their businesses next to the railway stations.

Hundreds of times, it has rained on the barren plateau; hundreds of times, the nostalgic mist has sunk into it, floating aimlessly in the sea of whiteness; and hundreds of times, one hears the cry of a worker falling into the abyss attracted by the eyes of the murky fog or the purple light of the sunset.

Morley's order rumbles when colliding with the solid rocks. In this way, it turns the work into the most difficult railroad in the world. Regardless of Harman's opinion and Alfaro's approval, he should comply with Leonidas Plaza and Morley's order. They point out the new direction of the train although later all economic calculations that the work demands are fantastic. They do not even suspect the approximate high costs, but they know that there is the possibility that the work may remain unfinished, which would be a political failure for Alfaro.

The ex-president listens attentively to what is happening with his great work, in which he placed all his hopes. In any case, because of Plaza's decision to take over the railway, he could not do anything. His former student no longer listens to him. And to think that if Leonidas Plaza won this honorable seat, it was because Alfaro ran him as a candidate and lent him a hand so that he would ascend to power.

Working around the clock, they now raise containment and channel walls from the Pazán River—which is overflowing in the vicinity of Huigra, covering much of the railway line, and seriously affecting the company.

The site now looks strange and eerie. The workers observe it with sadness, and they think that it is the devil's fault. The sky, covered in gray clouds, weighs somberly. The waters of the Chanchán River threaten to overflow, so they quickly build a provisional pipeline to pump 40,000 liters of gasoline and thus avoid shortages in the country.

In the distance, the covered mountains gleam like a gigantic white cloak from which falls an icy breath and where, in the evenings, bonfires soar, fires shimmering in the darkness. Sometimes they hear a guitar that sings nostalgically. The astonished laborers contemplate the landscape; it is as if they had arrived in an extinct astral landscape. They will need to move along those roads, discover horizons, and climb heights which are carpenters of shadows and where angst is felt and loneliness cries tirelessly.

They continue the task. They advance toward the heights only in the company of the wild and incomprehensible singing of the cold and strident wind that blows in the mountains. John Karruco, after hearing Gregory moan, comes to massage his legs and wrap them with leaves to warm them so that he can continue his assignment. Everyone has a good reason to move forward. It is an example of Alfaro's strength and that of Harman Davis, who was a teacher on the railway line with a three percent incline; his achievement takes on the characteristics of a miracle. With his engineer and surveyor's skill and ability, he becomes a genius with patience; and with unwavering foresight, he persists for months looking for a conscientious and more responsible, more suitable, and safer trail for the line. He is in no hurry; he does not rush out obeying an impatient desire. He can't rely on luck, which is why he never randomly delivers the choice of the multiple routes. He seeks to explore all of the possibilities to find the best, the truest, and the safest route that does not indicate some risks for travelers.

Engineer Bennett's words cause a deep silence: with a slow and monotonous voice, he advises the laborers that they should blast the rocks with dynamite at the site of *La nariz del diablo*. The laborers look with amazement at the summit, and noting the Jamaicans' fear, Bennett continues his chat. He says that he has taken a place in the course of history in the past few years. "These huge rocks," he says, "are hampering the development of the work, and you will need to blast through them."

It is necessary for the chosen laborers to be proud of what they are going to perform because to a worker, it is a great honor to carry out one of the more technical and important tasks of the project. The chosen ones cannot refuse; it is their duty to fulfill their promise of hard work.

All of the attention and concentration should be on the explosive material. A laborer possesses courage, discipline, and responsibility in handling bars, drills, gunpowder, and dynamite. He assures them that the work is very simple; it only requires precision, skill, and a bit of good luck. It is a question of throwing the stick of dynamite in the site to ensure that the rock explodes into pieces. It requires mental concentration and looking at the target well.

The Marret brothers look at each other; then they look at the engineer, who smiles while he explains the coordination of movements necessary to avoid being hit by dynamite. When the rugged rocks of *La nariz del diablo* fall into the abyss, it will pave the way to route the railway line.

At the end of his lecture, he notices Gregory and Syne, who do not dare to hold his gaze, because they believe that he is the devil.

They seem to have understood that they have just been selected to carry out the dangerous assignment, and they know that they must comply with the order. They imagine placing the stick of dynamite with the lit fuses and then the rocks flying through the air. They feel chills, and sadly, they obey.

The younger of the Marret brothers swears to himself in order not to think of the danger or even for what he has been selected. In those moments, he remembers his children and Pamela, his wife, who begged him not to leave them alone. He tries not to think about the dynamite, so he imagines Edna and David playing in the hut while their mother sells fruits in the streets.

He works nonstop on the assigned task, but he goes back to thinking about his family; he wants to hug them. To date, he has some savings although not enough to buy the land where his house would be built. He wonders if they will pay him more for carrying out the most dangerous job. He assumes that when the railroad work is done, they will parade through the streets of Quito. The army band will lead the march; and from the balconies, they will throw flowers, and they will cheer them, and they will march proudly. "They will give us a gold medal, and the supervisor will tell us that we are heroic laborers who have faced so many dangers because of the railroad," he thinks and smiles emotionally.

Lost in his thoughts, he forgets about the dynamite and the terrible fear of having it in his hands. He looks at the sky as if asking for help. He is afraid of falling or of being mutilated. He feels a mixture of sensations that breaks the wall of his tranquility. It paralyzes him and makes him swallow saliva to suppress the tears that are on the verge of jumping out of him. He moves his head to analyze what is going on. He waits to be officially designated by Bennett. It would not serve anything to discuss it in these moments because Wio is a man of stone, who in Harman's absence has accentuated his usual impenetrability; he shows no reaction—not even a greeting or an expression of surprise. Standing with his arms crossed, he stares in an expressionless manner.

If he now talks to the laborers, it is because he has no other alternative since he must persuade them about the benefit of the changes made to the tracking route. Among those appointed are the Marret brothers and John Karruco. Gregory is quiet for a few minutes, the time required to recover a little mental balance; and he thinks that someday his family will come to visit this place, and they will see his name and that of their uncle engraved on a plaque, and proudly they will say "how brave my father and my uncle were," and their black eyes will glow with happiness.

He does not think about the dynamite. He stops himself from thinking about anything so as not to get nervous. He does not even think about the fact that he was selected because he is one of the larger-sized workers; he should be satisfied because he is one of the best. He smiles.

At certain times, he would have preferred to be considered a bad worker to avoid having to confront this responsibility; he would now be worry free. He regrets having come to Ecuador; he never thought that there could be so much danger. Since the time he was selected as the blaster, he can't get rid of the anxiety.

At night, when lying down on his pallet, he has the impression of carrying the stick of dynamite in his hands with the fuse lit. When he thinks about it, he feels fatigue and weariness. While he is asleep, just one thought occupies his mind: dynamite.

The Marret brothers and other selected workers are ready to blow up the rocks. Their whole body shakes; they do not think of anything else but throwing the dynamite and escaping as fast as possible before the explosion reaches them. They spend hours reviewing the procedure. The members of the group are good-looking, robust, and agile men. All wait in complete silence. They receive special provisions for the progress of the task. Gregory clenches his teeth; he addresses his brother, asking him to take care of his family in case he fails. Turning his head, Syne makes a sign that he accepts; and he runs toward his brother. He hugs him and tells him that everything will work out well.

They all get ready. They drill the rocks on which they place the stick of dynamite strapped to a rope, which they will ignite to blow up the rock. The first to go is Gregory, who before the operation remains in deep silence; he meditates and prays to God. All eyes are riveted on him. The action requires courage and valor. The forces appear to be disrespectful to him. He knows that his body is weakened, but his honor pushes him to move forward. At stake is his homeland. "I am Jamaican," he thinks. He waits for the inevitable moment.

He knows that in this story, there are many slaughtered. Syne, jittery, is about to break into tears. He wants to hug his brother. He stops. He fears that he is never going to see him alive again. His breathing is agitated, time goes by slowly, and a strange movement makes his hands shake. There is a collective anxiety; everyone covers their ears because of the noise that the explosion will produce.

Everything that happens seems unlikely. They fear a catastrophe, and despair is the general thinking. They listen to the birds sing. A small error—just a small error—would cause a disaster and then would come the mourning. Gregory thinks only of success. His children will be proud of him, and he removes from his mind all negative thoughts; he forgets the danger. He pulls out strength. He wants to become a hero but one who is alive. These reflections give him courage.

He hits the target, the blast is heard, and it is already far away.

Iguanas, squirrels, and birds retreat. They fly to hide in the thickest part of the jungle. Many are hit by the explosion, and they fall into dust forever. Gregory reaches the other side, stunned and confused. Always loyal to the project, he has only one goal: the work of the railway. He recognizes that to build on the rock is very difficult.

A cold sweat slides down his face and his back. He puts his hand over his eyes to remove the sweat that clouds his view. He jumps to an open space and falls face forward, cursing Bennett out loud. He lets off steam, and his hoarse echo collides with the rocks.

Gregory's feat is discussed in the camps, and he receives cheers since it is a real triumph to know how to handle dynamite; it is not simply a matter of strength but of skill and luck. One must have a good pulse and a good aim though. The accomplishment fills him with pride.

Already in doña Miche's canteen, they lift up a glass of brandy; and they toast Gregory's success. He will remember all his life his valor at that time. But the dangers have not ended; this time he was saved, and he wonders when the construction of the railway line will be complete. This thinking takes over everyone and produces a dense silence. There is concern; they do not have peace of mind, of spiritual strength to resist the danger.

They celebrate the adventure, but they mix sadness with joy. They are left to carry it under the torrents of enthusiasm. They sing in unison Jamaican melodies to the beat of the drum and the guitar played by John Karruco. Syne sighs for Leona; he regrets having let her leave.

Gradually they are forgetting their sorrows, the dangerous tasks, and the tragedies; and they unite with the enthusiasm of remembering that they are Jamaicans. They do not lack anecdotes, legends, and memories of Lamboreo. They leave the canteen laughing aloud. John Karruco is the happiest of the group. He looks at the sky, and like a petrified man in the middle of the street with a bottle in one hand, he shouts "damn dynamite." And then between hiccups, he affirms that there are two types of rays: one from the moor and the other from the warm earth. The villagers make him promise not to make any further damage to nature. He accepts and goes off to die in peace.

It is said that one day, they proposed to measure their strength, to find out who is the strongest. The Moor beam presumes to be the most vigorous because he feeds on potatoes, corn, carrots, and soy; and he appears before the rain. The Earth beam faces his enemy and claims to be the strongest because he feeds on seafood, fish, bananas, and cassava. The battle is very long. They mutually toss sparks and lightning, and the damage they do to the earth is of great proportions. Tired, they retire. One day as the Earth beam is walking by the Moor, he discovers that his enemy is asleep; and he curses him so that in the next encounter, he will defeat the Moor beam. The people, frightened, assemble and decide to investigate who the Earth beam is; and they discover that he is an old man who is afraid of the green pumpkin and who walks supported by a gold cane. One day they steal the cane from him and bring it back to a pumpkin. The old man, frightened, goes to the people and asks for forgiveness for the damage caused to the earth.

The group of friends goes through an alley. Syne confesses that he is in love with Leona, groaning as he is reminded of her. Now they move to where the Asians are, who had been the first to arrive to settle along the railway line. The Marret brothers, because of the glasses of alcohol they consumed, begin to imitate mister Chun San Julio Wong, Congking Wong, and the popular Chail—the owner of a bakery that sells bread made of water, sugar, egg, and cinnamon with ginger, and various types of sweets. The group feels honored by the ritual that Asians have a tendency to receive them: the grace to bend and to join their hands at their chest as a means of greeting them while their eyes shine, and they smile with elegance.

The group continues until they find a sandlot, and they sit down to breathe the scent of freshly cut poplar. John Karruco stretches his legs. He is heard crying, but no one knows if it is from pain or fear or sadness or (maybe) joy. His eyes flood with tears. The light wind mixes the smell of the mountains with the forest and the jungle. It is the fresh aroma that brings to him in one fell swoop the presence of his parents, and as if he were reading a book, he begins to tell of his family's misery: the blindness of his father and his two brothers. John remains still and says that he can never marry. "I'm afraid that my children may also be blind. It is a curse that persists and haunts me." His great inner drama floats up with the heroic love for his family. In his grapelike and weeping skin, he shelters the nostalgia that his father and his brothers leave for him, whom he remembers as a miracle of light in his solitude. He thinks that later, maybe the next day, they will return to place a stick of dynamite and will quickly escape so that splinters do not reach them afterward.

Rain falls in thick drops. The morning has become dark, wrapped in a ghostly atmosphere. The birds chirp frightened, and suddenly, as if they had seen a ghost, terror takes hold of them; and they leave terrified, trampling themselves. The usual silence of the camps is transformed into a buzz. The branches of the trees are moving, and nobody knows why.

In unison, the birds scream and seek refuge thus defending themselves from something or someone. They flee nervous and get to the camps. The noise is unbearable and unusual. The laborers with wide-open eyes observe the spectacle without understanding the birds' behavior.

The scene attracts Burns Mackenzie's attention (who manages very well, even without support), and he intends to discover the cause of the phenomenon. He is concerned because since childhood, he has been interested in investigating rare events.

Without a doubt, something or someone has frightened the birds. Patiently he enters the forest. He sharpens his ears and his nose, and he follows the opposite direction of the flight of the frenzied birds. *But where has the unknown and frightening character come from?*

The squeaking intersects in the morning darkness. Mackenzie slowly follows where his intuition takes him. He crosses a path while looking at all the sides and the tops of the trees. Pensive, he sits down to wait until he sees in the tallest part of the tree an owl which emits squawks; and it defends itself from the light by closing its eyes. It has confused the night with day.

To Burns, such a discovery is worth the right to spend a night with a girl from the brothel, which is located on the outskirts of the town. It would not be the first time that they used the horse to go for fun.

"I'm not going."

"Why? Let's go dancing."

"I've never enjoyed a woman. I seldom go to those places."

"You're young."

"I've only had three girls. I don't have the experience that all of you have, and the previous times, I haven't enjoyed myself because of the fear of diseases and because it makes me sad for the girls."

"You have to try hard."

The hall is lighted by two kerosene lamps. Some couples dance to the beat of guitars and violins, instruments of fashion. When they arrive, two young women with low-cut necklines receive them. They sit at the back of the hall and drink beer.

On hearing the music with the rhythm of a waltz, one of the girls gets Burns to dance; and they whirl around the dance floor with the Jamaican's grace. After dancing to several selections, they embrace; and while he caresses his dance partner's cheeks, he says loving words in her ear. The light goes out. At that moment, Burns imagines that he is in danger of dying.

"Stop, you bastard! This woman is mine, dammit."

A man threatens him with a machete. Burns begins to sweat cold. He is stripped of his drunkenness; he has felt fear before, a distinct fear. But this one has a machete near his neck, and it is shining in the dark. It makes him wet his pants.

"Turn on the light! The light!"

The girl takes him by the hand, and they hide under a table. Burns will often remember this episode.

Economist Bennett plots as if it were a war. Now, the laborers toil more fearfully as they pierce the belly of a mountain. They work with picks, shovels, and machetes. Eager to finish, they put up with torrential rains; however, technicians do not consider that the weight of the mountain is giving way. This worries Syne, who is gifted with great perception, because he has experience in those jobs. He notices that from the upper walls of the mountain, stones are gliding ever more frequently. He tells the technicians what is happening, but they say that what is occurring is normal.

They continue extracting land and forming mounds so that other laborers take it up to the side of the road.

Concerned, Syne looks up; he has the feeling that the mountain is collapsing. He feels vertigo. The fear of being buried alive shakes him. At the same time, he warns that an avalanche of dirt, mud, and stones is falling on the laborers. The Jamaican uses his ability of defense and solidarity in such dangerous circumstances, and before the avalanche sheds its long shadow over other friends, he gives the cry of alarm. He breaks ranks, and he anticipates it; and in a quick maneuver, he pushes them toward the exit. The mouth of the cave is narrow. All run until the collapse reaches them. They understand that the situation is dangerous. The laborers, nervous and confused, go in despair toward the exit. Some, who are dazed, raise their arms, hoping to be saved. It produces an overrun; some slip, others cling to the closest companion, and those that fall in the mud are crushed. They are all afraid of dying buried.

They push themselves, and they step back; in the darkness, they have lost their sense of direction. They move, they organize within a broad frontline of fire, and they start an engulfing movement that does not allow them to run. In that chamber, everyone shouts at the same time. They all make an effort to abandon the place, and they have to cover a long stretch.

The slide throws trees and stone; and Syne, because of helping his friends, is caught by a large root that fractures his leg. He only manages to get out thanks to his brother Gregory for his help.

This time many workers remain buried as it is impossible to rescue them because of the great size of the avalanche. Terror takes over from the tragedy. Between sobs, screams, and moans, the men swear not to return to work on the railway.

The pain of losing their friends is so deep that they run terrified on hearing the noises emitting from the mountain. Stunned, there are plenty who are thrown into the void.

For the Jamaicans, the mountain took revenge for being wounded because its honeycomb of sweetness has been wounded. They have injured its rest and its living heart. They have killed the joy of the birds of the forest, the majesty of the Andes. All of the survivors move away from the labyrinth of mud; and rain explains to them, crying, that it possesses a rebellious spirit.

The builders are facing the problem of desertion by the laborers, the reason why they focus their attention on the "facts."

They do not stop the work; it continues where rocks form skyscrapers. The wind dismisses a faint cry, dawn's fog weeps, and not even the birds manage to leave footprints. There is a need to continue drilling the rock. Now it is John Karruco's turn. He is searching in the crate for a stick of dynamite, and then he sips a drink of brandy to soothe his nerves.

A small and weak ray of sunshine seeps into the atmosphere. John thinks that if Gregory was successful, he also will be. He can catch that incomprehensible charm of the rock if he does not proceed quickly.

The actions of mechanism are the same in all cases. He mentally repeats the scene again and again until it is well memorized.

There it is, stubbornly—the rock of *La nariz del diablo*, an unmistakable wall because of its excessive slope and where the railway line will cross. The workers still consider the absurdity of having changed the route of the Nelly track that connects Huigra with Sibambe, across the Chanchán track with the dangers of the river.

After a long silence, John Karruco sees the signal and is ready to proceed; but suddenly, the lighted stick of dynamite comes loose and strikes him.

The workers watch the act with anguish and horror; they scream, they sweat cold, and between moans, they coordinate the rescue. Some throw themselves on the grass. They shout in the middle of John's agonizing moan. The horrible circumstances produce penetrating pain. All that now remains of the railway work that would climb *La nariz del diablo* is disenchantment and disillusionment. Every day death comes.

The laborers stand up; they protest angrily, for it is a very strong blow that they have received. For a long time, the armed police struggle to pacify the laborers. Syne grips Engineer Bennet by his hair. He shakes his head back and forth, and he hits him in the chest and drops him. When Bennett's body hits the grass, he spits at him. The workers look at the fallen man on the ground, and when Syne hears a cry, he turns his head. It is Gregory, who separates his brother, before the guards shoot him.

Badly injured, John Karruco is taken to the campsite to be attended by Dr. Arroyo. He is unconscious. Pain blocks his brain; and immobile, with open eyes, he refuses to close them. He sees bright fragments of dynamite in his field of vision. Blood soaks his body and is gradually abandoning him. He has cold feet. He has lost both arms.

Overwhelmed by the tragedy, workers protest the lack of safety as they are caught in an invisible spider's web around the railway. Bennett walks nervously amid the noisy crowd, and with uncertain words, he tries to calm the situation down; however, he does not get the desired peace, and they accuse him of being the cause of the misfortune.

Fearing a strike, he decides to seek the help of President Plaza Gutiérrez, who has doubled the surveillance to preserve order and to force the workers to return to their jobs. Since then, the President routinely carries out periodic visits to personally observe the progress of the work.

They put their doubts aside. Bennett exerts a great deal of influence over Plaza. It seems incredible to them that a man of such high authority maintains relationships with a realtor. They shelter the hope that the presidency will return to don Eloy Alfaro. This will occur much later, but for now, the work climate is more rigid; nevertheless, the disturbances continue, a sign of great discontent. On taking a look at the past and upon remembering don Eloy, they say that it is an honor for Jamaicans to serve in Ecuador, to deliver their efforts to Alfaro, the man who has the most daring dreams and who set his sights on the railway arriving to Quito.

Because of the route change, violent accidents are produced that will hereafter remain in the shadow of the days. Meanwhile, among the brethren, each time a more spiritual, patient, and organized escalation of historical action is studied in depth.

At dusk, workers stop eagerly to observe the progress on the railway line; they understand that they are defeating social injustice and that there is no time to lose; that someday Ecuadorians will remember their sacrifices and that they were laborers with nerves of steel.

One can barely distinguish the silhouette of another, so absolute is the darkness of the clouds. They think about the return of don Eloy. For them it is important and necessary.

Poverty, weariness, and sadness drag John Karruco by the strength of his inertia. He searches for a reason to continue living. His voice breaks and the words end in a suffocating gurgle. He firmly turns his view with a look of amazement that slowly transforms into a certainty: death.

Silent and melancholic, enclosed in his grim imperviousness, he continues to suffer. He cannot resign himself to having lost his arms. With feelings already numb, he no longer desires to live; and with a weak and gaunt face, he does not support the misfortune with valor. Engineer Bennett considers that it was bad luck but that not everyone will have the same fate.

The noise of the dynamite, the blows of jackhammers, and the tolling of the rails is constant; and John identifies it with unending sadness.

They listen to new cries and new explosions; dynamites continue to produce new losses, whose jobs are occupied by others. Those who lose an arm, a leg, or an eye are evacuated to another kind of task. The builders do not listen to any requests or claims; they are there to finish the railway line without any contract of responsibility.

Authorities report the developments to the President through daily telegrams that are sent to him. So Plaza knows all the details about the progress of the route, which gradually spreads like an iron snake.

Rain returns to cause landslides and to take advantage of what is left. The task is restarted. A great deal of money is invested, and there is debt to be cancelled; so it is necessary to make an effort until the end and keep the peace. They cannot entangle themselves in sorrow or put up a fight against nature.

Moral anguish overcomes the laborers, and worry takes away their tranquility. In the camp, comments and rumors of all sorts are flowing; and whether it is hope, despair, or sadness, every time they see that there are fewer companions to work on the railway, it is because it has swallowed them alive. The Jamaicans struggle against the temptation to surrender. They are tormented by the responsibility that they acquired, along with the disenchantment and the danger.

In the history of the railways, none had required greater energy or intelligence in order to conquer so many natural obstacles. And there are many reasons to state that the railway line has confirmed the workers' deaths and that nature presents a noble rematch; it defends itself and, at many times, expresses revenge.

These arguments are used by the workers—who, with holy humility in their eyes, raise a prayer for the fallen in the company. When the evening invents silence, Gregory calls roll aloud of all the colleagues who rest forever in these places. It is when a long moan sounds under the starry sky. They retreat through a tunnel of sadness.

With each tragedy, survivors hold each other's hands. With eyes moist from tears and with trembling lips, they lift up a prayer. The tragedy establishes a halt in the construction of the road. Wrinkles accentuate them and the soul is saddened. The authorities erase the names of the deceased from their lists without shedding a single tear.

No one remembers having known such a terrifying silence. There are times when the wind is silent, and everyone is even afraid of his shadow. Life along the railway, as stations are established, suffers an impact due to the number of inhabitants. The shadow of the peasants gathers on the roads.

Each one now works tirelessly, and the zigzag in *La nariz del diablo* is a reality. For Morley, the layout is infallible. They have risen to the powerful, perfect, and strange, mountaintop, where silence and a fragrant of the Andean solitude drink from a glass. One feels like a wind god. The railway line is inventing an alphabet with which the depth of time is read, but it is also a huge snake showing its forked tongue with an evil blood. It shows the world an avenue of volcanoes, a life filled with shades of green, a wind with a jungle smell, a solitary step filled with pleasure, geography of loneliness.

The Jamaicans absorb the wonder that they are gradually building; they can no longer hide their admiration, nor can they curb their enthusiasm. It has cost them effort, sweat, and blood.

At night, sitting beside the road, they talk, cry, and laugh. Around the campfires, they are filled with astonishment and dismay on realizing that the train ascends *La nariz del diablo* making a zigzag. A cruel and sinister memorial site for the peasants, a site twisted by intimate torture on the spine of the mountain range, and that it rises to heaven to sniff the air of the constellations.

The shadows multiply the noise of the locomotives that rapidly cross populated dreams. It extinguishes the smile of the lonely when the train's whistle escapes from the mountain pass.

Time doesn't stop; it passes over *La nariz del diablo*, and the laborers press on to the opening trails. The goal is to reach Chimbacalle, the last station. It begins to draw ever clearer the significance of the railway. New perspectives are opened. It is a situation that will change the living conditions of the country, the general state of the spirit of the people, and the relationships between coastal and highland areas.

Opponents of Alfaro are silenced; they cannot deny the change. They see the nation's economy growing, and they forget for a few months the ungrateful claim that the railway is the messenger of atheism.

The passengers never before dreamed of feeling the strange and exceptional beauty of the Andes. The air and the sun salute the presence of the railway. Tenderness opens up to a new world; the Ecuadorians' existence acquires other dimensions. It has discovered a prodigious wildlife, an inexhaustible mine of landscapes, a thousand trails that lead to the most secret joy.

The workers continue receiving orders. "Open trails, place sleepers, and lay rails." Syne limps when walking; it is the sad memory that he has of when the mountain slid. The crew continues as the night disappears, and the workers go in shifts to rest. Gregory cries inconsolably. With the weeping, he expresses a desire to begin the journey back home. Suddenly, the memory brings to him Pamela's fleshy lips on the frontier of the wind; and in the evening, he falls asleep. Perhaps he sheds drops of semen on baring his heart.

The Trans-Andean Railroad has produced transformations in the Jamaicans. Some of the mutilated men want to stay in Ecuador: those who have lost their arms, feet, eyes, hands, and lungs can no longer return to their country and are hopeful that the authorities will give them a pension to subsist, in recognition of their great sacrifices. Such generosity is perfectly justified. They will insist until justice favors them; otherwise, the authorities may not rest peacefully because thousands of voices will disturb their dreams. The image of the mutilated and their cries will pursue them without rest.

The hills surrounding the stations acquire, under the setting sun, a violet tone that glistens in some and is hardly visible in others. They cross summer clouds whose colors constantly change.

From the moment that the day dawns and the sun appears, the clouds that have formed fantastic countryside dissipate and leave the sky cloudless.

On a Sunday afternoon—full of conversations, laughter, and jokes that they exchange between themselves—the laborers comment that they hope to see don Eloy very soon, at the inauguration of the Guamote Station. Alfaro has been invited along with his family.

What makes Hugh's heart happy is the complicity of the workers to take time and practice what they all call football. There are no rivals; respect and friendship are retained. What would it have been to mix hatred in all this? Spencer celebrates the deeds performed by his peers. The twenty-two players arouse emotions in public, jumping from happiness.

Delightfully they are victorious. Each one speaks and writes about the match. Sadness and nostalgia are eased. And that activity and the Jamaicans' energy make the authorities think that it has been a superb idea to bring laborers from that country. They observe so many qualities in them: they are beings of action and are tough, joyful, and optimistic men. True, very close. They are hardworking; and their strength stands out—not for suffering from nervous disorders—but they know how to cope with loneliness, the terrible loneliness that sometimes one feels to see only the rain. Such fortitude makes them superior to feelings as overwhelming as depression and sadness.

Cries are heard coming from the field. The green T-shirts have won, and they celebrate the victory with an uproar.

"It would be convenient to send Spencer to Durán Station as manager."

"I agree," accepts the boss. "Taylor should also go."

The facts follow the words. A week later, Hugh and Taylor arrive to the province of Guayas.

Guamote (golden by the sun), sown willows, and *capuli* trees[9], await Alfaro's arrival—he who has forged the destiny of the railway. Since the early hours of the morning, they have waited to hear the whistle that will bring a plot of excitement. The heart of Guamote acquires new vigor, and its river reflects the innocent face of that Rocío region.

The inhabitants often ask themselves if all that wonder, all that exciting beauty, is nothing more than a dream. People talk about the success radiating above everything that makes it immortal. Houses are totally lit. They adorn them with garlands made with branches and flowers. A rosary of burners, lamps, and candles is arranged along the railway line. Happiness floats in the air.

It is necessary to welcome the "Monster of Steel," "the Black Marvel," "the Stubborn Animal," "the Irritating Locomotive," the Trans-Andean Railroad and Alfaro.

People chat, laugh loudly, walk at ease, eat tortillas with eggs, and drink *el morocho*.[10] A jovial dancer constitutes entertainment. A radical change is operating in the spirit and in the customs of the citizens.

---

[9] Capuli tree is a species of cherry tree, which can grow in much warmer weather than traditional cherries. It is believed to be native to Mexico, but was introduced to the Andes by the Spanish.

[10] El morocho, also called *morocho dulce*, is a thick sweet drink made with morocho corn, milk, cinnamon, sugar and raisins. Morocho is a classic Ecuadorian comfort drink and is primarily sold on the streets or at markets.

Guamote has to become the most important station; and the whole country should know the economic and strategic importance of this station, of its imminent connection with the capital of the Republic and with the other stations. Guamote continues to offer a very attractive and dynamic appearance. New businesses appear—jobs and sources of income for the population—as it develops in the railway terminal. It provides everything one may need for the maintenance of the trains: a building for the station with a waiting room, housing for employees, warehouses, etc.; detours for storage of carts, a "Y" to change direction of the locomotives, livestock; and a trench for the mechanical workshop.

Cries and agitation are produced. The people look with pride at the progress; a great part of the population acquires land on which to build houses, restaurants, and hotels. New commercial premises are opened like that of the Italian Romeo Nelly, of the Peruvians José Domingo Quiñónez and Luis Jiménez, and of another large number of traders from the province of Guayas.

The city expands and is modernized. The inhabitants of Guamote speak with authority and with the air of experts. A lot of money runs through their hands. And that place, lost in the mountain range, which nobody talked about because it was unknown to all, happens to appear in the statistics of the country.

It is the Trans-Andean Railroad. The inhabitants of the place for the first time feel that they have found a way to earn an income and an occupation. In the course of time, the prices of goods and necessities are experiencing a boost. One earns a lot of money that is circulating, and there is employment for the majority of the inhabitants. The cash is kept under the mattress or in chime boxes. Without a doubt, some families are making a fortune; and the world of night owls increases.

At nightfall, the streets take on an air between somber and mysterious as a cold wind runs without finding refuge. In the sky, the stars smile; and the god of joy turns on the heart of the night owls. Customers with money go to the bars and to clandestine places.

With brandy, projects trample each other since being employed on the railroad or starting their own business. They know that to have money, one just needs luck. People make everything else. Already drunk, they say that luck only comes if one earns it.

The crowd awaits the arrival of Alfaro; nobody wants to miss the opportunity to welcome him, to join the chorus of the people who are now smiling at the prospect of a better destiny. New families arrive— the Avilés, Zuritas, Palacios, Jaramillos, Argüellos, Armijos—which form very leafy genealogical trees.

Rosa Kaviedes' room is located on a very steep slope toward Los Laureles Street. From there one can see the plaza, the church, and the park. Burns Mackenzie goes up in a hurry, he sticks out his tongue from time to time and makes an "ugh" to express his tiredness.

The house is surrounded by trees and a garden filled with daises; and white, pink, red, and even purple roses. The Jamaican walks in big strides, intermixing what he sees with the things that are in his thoughts; and he attempts to organize them in the best way to high-light the love that he has for Rosa. Once, twice, three times, he repeats his proposal of marriage. He makes an effort, but he still fails to focus on the main idea.

He progresses slowly. Being there encourages him so often that he has ended his relationship with the young woman only to return with more intensity. In short, love becomes ruthless and painful as it is characteristic of all true love, which hurts and cuts in order to grow and take shape.

His words mingle with accents of hope, appeal, and fear. He is afraid that he is not ready to get married. He fails to give impetus to his ideas. "But I imagine Rosa. I see her in my dreams. I built my house for her because I will bring her to live with me. I'll buy a big bed . . . I think of her. I count the days. Yes, I will marry Rosa, but if I propose to her . . . we could . . . I could tell her to come live in my house and then get married. No, she is not going to give in . . . she is a virgin, and she will not take off her clothes," he sighs. There is no other bond that formalizes the commitment. "I will marry Rosa Kaviedes."

The city is celebrating because the Old Warrior is coming to share his desire to see the arrival of the railroad. People are alert; everyone wants to remember that moment to tell it to their children and to their grandchildren. They haven't even opened the shops and other businesses. It is a day of joy, and they wish to express their gratitude to don Eloy. To tell him aloud that he is the manager of the Trans-Andean Railroad.

The announcement is made that his arrival will be in the morning. It makes the railway terminal fill with shouts, praises, songs, and dances. They remain vigilant, but the hours pass and he does not appear. No person enjoys such great respect and considerations of the people as Alfaro. People see in him the prototype of a good-hearted, serene, and courageous soul.

Slowly, townspeople move away, walking toward their homes; and they meditate at the same time about the absence of don Eloy. Normalcy returns to the city, and the railroad did not arrive.

However, that night, a long whistle that crossed the border of silence is heard. A gigantic crowd abandons their homes in the middle of the uproar; and general commotion already dominates in the terminal, in the streets, and in the squares. The people greet Alfaro, who has arrived with his family and Lamboreo. Everyone again listens to the whistle, and cheerfulness is the norm.

"Long live Alfaro, dammit!"

"Long live the Old Warrior!"

"May he live long! May he live long! May he live long!"

He raises his arms to greet them. To everyone it seems impossible to see the man so closely who, filled with tenderness, smiles—so closely. In those moments, emotion is the norm. It is something great and rare. In the eyes of the people, something is happening that seems unlikely. A reality so wonderful. Each one in turn wants to be near him.

They shout for joy, and everyone has left their homes to meet don Eloy and the railroad. They remain engrossed in watching the train. They don't understand what they are seeing; some think that it must be an invention of the devil (especially the black men who man it).

Suddenly, Lamboreo jumps up; and his and Syne's shouts and hugs draw attention. How far it is from Lamboreo to imagine that the skinny man without arms who is looking at him with profound sadness is John Karruco, converted into a humble fish with fins, a mutilated brother, a beggar for water, a fragment of nothing more than a pitcher, a collapsed heap that does not seem to be alive but decaying like a buried stake!

"John!" he yells to him, and he hugs him frantically squeezing him.

"Lamboreo, Brother" he responds with a subdued voice, lowering his head.

Both have eyes full of tears.

"Damn dynamite . . ."

He moves as if he were a beggar, and he drags along the ground without stopping his tears.

Immediately after the arrival of the railway, while some advance step by step to touch it, others run to climb on it; and some remain beside it to examine it closely, without understanding how so big an apparatus can run as fast as a deer. For many, the railroad launches pitiful and prolonged moans while for others, it is a song of joy.

People beam, and in the midst of their tears, they do not hide their gratitude for Alfaro. Never before in Guamote has something similar and with such significance happened. Now everything is connected to the railway; and because of the inauguration, there have been politicians, journalists, traders, and prostitutes present. All have come to inaugurate the Guamote station. They consider that it is a fact that it gives the people privileges.

As representatives of President Leonidas Plaza Gutiérrez, some Ministers of State—who will inform the highest authority about the affection, veneration, and gratitude that the people feel for Alfaro—are present. There is the Guamote Station—which will be used not only to promote tourism or activate the economy, but also and most importantly to bring to them the alphabet, schools, books, and notebooks. It comes to sow the field of knowledge.

The people regain their breath. Now they are focused on the moment in which the train, full of merchandise and tourists, whistles announcing its arrival. People run, jump, and shout.

"Tortillas with eggs!"

"*Morocho, morocho!*"

It is the station's inaugural party, and all night, there are festivities that extend into several days. People come from different parts of the country. They also come to get acquainted with the church that the priests have built. They say that it is to counteract the atheism that will arrive with the train.

In the midst of joy and confusion, John Karruco notices in the people's eyes the same ruthless chain that expresses a question as if to say a single word: dynamite. Although he would like to forget his tragedy, to not be viewed with pity, and to not fall down with or without the devil in a dream or in reality, the truth is that he has lost both arms and that he, like thousands of other workers, is linked to the history of the railroad.

For the occasion, the Jamaicans have prepared "the railroader's stew" under John's direction. The stew is very popular among the railroad workers; and this time, Syne and Gregory have made it, taking advantage of the steam from the train's machinery. They have placed special care since they will toast don Eloy and his family. That is why they rush to get everything ready: tenderized beef, potatoes, carrots, leek, green pepper, salt, and pepper. The popular Chinese, Chail, donates white wine and olive oil to them.

Under Karruco's direction, Gregory cuts onions and garlic into julienne strips and reserves them. He cleans the carrots and leeks in little slices. He cleans and cuts the peppers into strips, and he cuts the potatoes into large chunks. He cuts the meat into pieces in order to make a stew.

In a pan, he sautés the onion and garlic in the olive oil on a low heat. When the onion is transparent, he adds the pieces of meat, salt, and pepper and also sautés everything on a low heat; then he adds the leeks, carrots, peppers, bay leaf, and white wine. He boils everything with the meat and onion, and when it is tender, he adds potatoes covering with water; and he adds salt.

Smiling and happy, Syne makes rice to go with the stew as he hopes to surprise the Alfaro family. During dinner, don Eloy's voice is heard, showing his joy to see part of his dream fulfilled at the opening of the station. He is happy to share with his family and with the people. He is in a good mood and does not hide his feelings. Next to him are Doña Anita, América, and Colón, who appreciate the people's kindness. In the comings and goings of the Jamaicans, praises from the attendees are heard about how delicious the stew and the rice are.

After dinner, no one can miss the toast for the Trans-Andean Railroad with a shot of brandy from the region. Doña Anita apologizes and gets up.

The Jamaicans are in the kitchen when they hear a woman's steps. They are surprised to see don Eloy's wife. Lamboreo, Gregory, and Syne greet her and stand up. The Panamanian lady is wearing a long sleeve suit with lace cuffs. Her hair looks pulled back in a bun, and her ears are adorned with shiny earrings. She has in her hands paper and pencil. She wants them to tell her how to prepare the railroader's stew. The Jamaicans smile, and Lamboreo gets a crate so that she can sit down. Syne is responsible for dictating the recipe to her. When the copying is complete, she expresses to them that she liked the stew very much.

In the meantime, don Eloy asks questions: sometimes to find out what people think about politics, other times to know about the behavior of the railway authorities. He has, however, a subtle way to find out because he deflects the subject with skill and seeks a justification that allows him to advance to the quick and pleasant chat full of anecdotes.

He is aware of everything, but he wants another kind of information. He listens to the workers about their feelings and their appreciation. He is worried about the business carried out by Economist Morley. He promises to cancel it if he returns to the presidency. This does occur in 1906, when Colonel Emilio Maria Terán rises in arms against President Lizardo Garcia Sorroza; and when the position becomes vacant, Alfaro assumes it.

It is his virtue to know how to narrate his experiences tinged with good humor. The attendees enjoy the expressions and picturesque comparisons that he uses, showing all his cultural background. When he speaks, men and women are silent as if they were in agreement. They listen to him with love and respect.

They are convinced that this great work sets off progress and happiness; wherever the railway passes, it carries light. *Mishguilli*, sweetness in Quichua, abandons its tortuous road from Puyal, Angostura, Salsipuedes, which the needy residents had to travel by mules who buried their hooves in the mud. The travelers raised their looks with the identical anguish, fearing the *Cuilca* and all that stood in its way.

The journey was difficult and complicated for them. They had questions and complaints that they frequently presented. Reasons and evidence were not lacking, but no one solved their problems because no authority remembered them.

It was a perilous adventure to travel on those deadly roads, and they were only stopping when unusual and extraordinary hunger was present. They calmed it with *máchica*,[11] *raspadura*,[12] and water that were there to drink; and then they returned to the flight.

People pronounce Alfaro's name with great joy. They feel committed to him; now new promises of loyalty surge with liberalism. They predict success and new victories for him.

They feel something big and exciting in their lives. They are linked to the Old Warrior through strong ties, and they openly promise to express their support for him.

"Long live Alfaro! Long live Alfaro!" shouts the crowd.

As he leaves, they carry him on a platform amid new cries of "Long live Alfaro! Long live liberalism! Long live the railroad."

And the sun, which prompts wonderful glimpses, is a witness to everything.

A month after the inauguration of the Guamote Station, the story of the opening is repeated but in reverse. Priests open a church, from whose pulpit they will inexorably fight the advance of liberalism.

Alfaro's political enemies, baffled by the new times they happen to live in with the railroad, don't come to exactly feel in a more accurate manner what their place is in the world. The huge iron machine, which moves at a high speed, has changed the perspective of time and of things.

For many hours, they remain in front of the ships that will carry the laborers back to Jamaica. Michael Sandiford, desperate, looks around him. He feels as if he only had one minute of life left; and he

---

[11] Máchica is a sweetened, spiced grain blend that Ecuadorans use to enrich the texture and flavor of drinks. Spanish colonists brought this cooking technique to Ecuador from Mexico, where corn is used instead of barley

[12] Unrefined raw sugar

holds his suitcase with one of his hands, waiting for his turn to board the ship. Luisa's attempt to hold him did nothing. Visibly troubled, he talks with his friends. Nervous, he senses something new that he has never felt before.

The word "return" now takes on a new meaning. He realizes that nothing—nothing of what he can say to his friends—would make them understand the attraction of returning to Jamaica because they believe that to return would be crazy.

Those who are staying promise to be peaceful and serene, but never was a vow so unfulfilled. At that time, the weather proves to be pleasant. The sea breeze blows strongly in the port of Guayaquil, where they have parallel ships to transport the workers.

Life, under its apparent complexity, is simple: sometimes the boat capsizes, but there is the possibility of saving it.

"We, who are staying, are some crazy men. The worst enemy that we have are ourselves."

Spencer, MacKenzie, Balket, Leona, and Syne, as if they were suddenly waking up from a nightmare, do some soul searching. They recover their balance, and they wonder, "And if we were to return? Would we be able to start over? Would we have courage?" Their legs are trembling. They all silently take each other's hands to feel solidarity. "Yemayá, give us courage!" exclaims Leona; and she shelters her son, Rigoberto.

At times they feel a shameful concern, a sort of tension. They suddenly falter. Memory, the past, and nostalgia all impose on their will to remain in Ecuador.

"Goodbye," says Michael Sandiford, and he embraces his friends. "Thank you. Thank you for everything." He moves toward the platform. But suddenly, he hears a girl crying that causes him a lively and unusual impression. He turns his face and sees his daughter in Luisa's arms. He comes back to reality to accept living the existence as it is and not a dream to become reality. He stays.

While most ships are moving away with the laborers, Syne's love for Leona is reborn more strongly in his heart. Forgetting about those present, they kiss.

"Goodbye," says Gregory, and he waves his arms.

They shut up. For a few moments, a flurry of sadness passes over all of the faces when they look at John Karruco, who raises his head as a farewell sign.

CHAPTER FOUR

*D*urán, June 23, 1908. A long whistle blowing, followed by two short ones, is heard in the depths of the jungle. The railway, which goes into the green heart of the Littoral, moves singing a long excitement; and then it passes through the solitude of the Andean mountain range, which looks like a stone cathedral.

"Long live Alfaro, dammit!"

"Long live Taita Alfaro!"

The crowd screams out; and joy is reflected on the faces of the inhabitants, who have left their jobs to welcome the train, which ignores all distances. It returns faith to life and returns joy like in a miracle.

The inhabitants of Yaguachi, Naranjito, Bucay, Huigra, Chanchán, Sibambe, Alausí, Tixán, Guamote, Riobamba, Ambato, Salcedo, Latacunga, Alóag, Tambillo—in short, the thirty stations that run along the railway—see the arrival of the train as a kind of light.

Machinist Bernardo Munisaga's[13] enthusiasm merges with the singing of the people and the birds—which, frightened, wonder what the mystery of that machine that runs so fast is—and, for a moment, grazes the loneliness.

---

[13] Arturo Munizaga was the engineer of the first train, locomotive #8, which made the inaugural trip.

The whistling in the wind is the same as that of the condor, which opens its wings in the celestial daylight. The "X" looks down over the rock, that long companion to the road. The wolf leaves his thirst on the banks of the Chanchán, between the shadows of summer, to hear the whistling that crosses the fields. "Long live Alfaro, dammit! Long live Taita[14] Alfaro!"

The railroad joyfully climbs the hills. It ascends the mountains that rise above the naked back of the valleys, and it climbs until it arrives where the condor reaches the height of the angels. In a zigzag, it reaches the top of the Andes since it cannot miss an appointment with Alfaro.

In the beginning, the idea of constructing that magical snake only had the flavor of the promise of a fable, and then it became a warm space. Like a shadow pursuing him, the railway represents his company. For him, the entire trip and all his travels are crossing on his imaginary train. The days pass, and the purpose of building it gives him no peace. The railway is the urgency of sleepless nights; all of his acts point toward that dream. His mind travels through inner clarities, taking refuge in burning silences. As a good freemason and leader, he clings to the faith, one which constitutes the starting point for a way of life and of a cosmo vision of the world around him. Faith is a practical philosophy that reaffirms the independence and originality to face the world, a philosophy that allows for the evolution of social relations.

He looks for balance between the old and the new to break with the political forces that have ruled with class and religious interests. "Long live the liberal revolution!" exclaims Lamboreo.

He feels the need to inspire the masses in a common sense expressed in the form of faith but a non-religious one, yet a national idea close to the unitary behavior of the proletariat.

Society demands that the mode of thinking en masse, without culture, be replaced with a common sense that will lead to changes in morality. The first engineer of the railway, Munisaga, convincingly said, "Long live the most difficult railway of the world!"

"Long may it live!" adds the crowd.

---

[14] Taita is an affectionate term meaning father

The long whistling, followed by two short ones, can clearly be heard; and the echo repeats it in the rugged mountain range. Those who are the closest run to meet "the Black Marvel" (as they have baptized it). For some, the whistle of the railway is a moan or a whine; for others, it resembles a human whimper; for still others, the train emits a kind of cry; for many, in the end, it is a song of joy.

In the villages, one hears praises in a loud voice; and one sees people who wave red bandanas as they greet the train. There is no one who does not feel trembling in his legs. With moist eyes and hands in the air, they shout. Nobody wants to miss the show or turn away from the view. Men and women run along the rail line, shaking the white hats of *toquilla* straw[15] in the air with a red headband. To the *alfaristas,* because of so much screaming, the veins in their necks pop out. Their eyes turn slowly but relentlessly. From their throats escapes a single expression, barely a few words. "Long live Al-fa-ro-o-o-o!"

The early morning smells like a forest of pine and eucalyptus. Quito is a girl once again, and she lights up her heart of clay. *El Panecillo* greets the light of that June 25, 1908; she welcomes the Trans-Andean Railroad.

At eight o'clock in the morning, the balconies in the Ecuadorian capital display flags and flowers; and to the chord of the national anthem, the flag of Ecuador is hoisted atop the government palace.

Alfaro leads the parade along with his ministers, diplomats, and members of the Supreme Court, the court of auditors, the superior court, and the board of the military committee. When the procession arrives at the Chimbacalle Station, excitement is the norm.

"The Black Marvel" makes its appearance. The first locomotive (number 12) greets the people of Quito with a long puff, which is answered with frenetic screams, "Long live the rail! Long live Alfaro!"

The clang of a canon is heard in *el Panecillo*. The locomotive moves forward until it is in front of President Alfaro; then he approaches the number 8, which also greets him with a long puff and takes the opposite line, allowing the people to board the train cars.

---

[15] *Toquilla* straw is the used to make the famous Panama hat, made in Ecuador.

The bells ring—in compliance with the decree of the Archbishop Federico González Suárez—every hour until ten in the evening. General Alfaro and his entourage are invited to enter the passenger cars of the machine number 12. Pedro Moncayo, Carlos Freile Zaldumbide, Octavio Diaz León, Archer Harman, and Flavio Alfaro greet the people; then, both trains move up to the point where the line crosses the road to Sangolquí, the point from which they return accompanied by machine number 10 that was stationed there.

From *El Panecillo*, the majestic walk of the three united machines can be seen, forming a single and extensive convoy that, on arriving back to the station, is received with thundering applause by the more than ten thousand people present there.

The Pichincha Volcano lights up with all its white robes. Silence comes suddenly. Alfaro, arm-in-arm with his daughter America, hammers in the last nail, a signal that the job is finished.

A girl from Daule gives a speech and adorns Alfaro with an artistic floral wreath. Representatives of institutions and associations of the country, after a series of speeches, deliver presents to the president, who responds to each one with few words.

He listens to don Amelio Puga, Minister of Public Works. "To one side, the shadows, indolence, hatred, laziness, ignorance, poverty. On the other hand, work, love, enthusiasm, science . . . What a difference from the past to the flattering present! Unite all the shoulders of goodwill! Let us draw near to the leader whose motto is 'honesty, freedom, and progress!'"

Dr. Abelardo Montalvo, president of the Council of Quito, says in a loud voice, "This is the redeeming work of Alfaro. Praise to Eloy Alfaro, who has been the heart and soul of railroad of the South. The most resounding anthem for him will be the hissing of the monster on the plateau of the Andes! Long live the Liberal Party."

The Old Warrior—that is the name given to the President for his persistence in the struggle, in spite of the defeats—wears his hair cut almost to snuff, and on his face are the apparent traces of the sun and combat. He greets them with his head high.

Many hours pass, and the people continue arriving to blend with the crowd; the railroad has filled the country with happiness. Shouts and chants resound. Now, don Eloy does not understand how he could have had people who opposed the project. Many times, when reading the press, he could not understand the words that were wounding his heart. It was a pain from an open artery. The press had campaigned against the construction of the railway and against the policy of the government.

"Long live Alfaro, dammit."

The opening of the railroad progresses and is covered with beauty. Humble faces stare, and a whisper runs all around. After so many years of unrest and uprisings—for the first time—peasants, workers, lay teachers, housewives, laundresses, and cooks all come together. *How long would this union last?*

The church hides its fear, but a series of excited voices and worried whispers come from the pulpits. The campaign against Alfaro is implied each time with more precision and clarity. The devil, they say to him. The Church is concerned about the triumph of the rebellions.

The rebellions maintain the civic fervor of earlier times. They fully comply with its imposed task in hopes of the changes offered by Alfaro.

"We have succeeded," said Pedro Moncayo when looking at this multitude.

Liberal leaders observe the sublime act. The government of the Old Warrior fundamentally understands dialectical methods, based on the reality—in the facts—and enriched with the political experience of the country and of Latin America. This is not an opposition to the Ecuadorian Church but of a process to find a meaning in the history, the alliance of the Church and the State determined by a monolithic worldview opposite to that of the indigenous, Blacks, and mestizos.

"Long live don Eloy! Long live!" shouts Lamboreo, and he lifts up Rigoberto so he can see the scene.

"Long live the Liberal Party!" exclaims Leona.

Everyone thinks that life will be fair with the railroad; it will open up new sources of work, and the country will enjoy a balance up to now unknown to them, a harmony to which all Ecuadorians aspire. The country will no longer be poor since the railway comes to embrace the sea with its orchestras as it embraces the Andes mountain range, holding a constellation of volcanoes on its chest.

"Long live the Old Warrior," say the people of Esmeraldas.

He listens to the swirling crowd that is shouting. At a distance, he sees the Jamaicans (Marret, Taylor, Mackenzie, Spencer, Sandiford), those from Esmeraldas, and those from Chotá. He knows them very well because they have worked on the railway line.

In the air, a mixture of smells is floating. A sense of triumph covers the environment. One-two, one-two, beats don Eloy's heart serenely, confidant and in a trance of wellbeing. The majority of his friends have been given an appointment along the railway tracks; and from the villages, where ever the train passes, they fall into euphoria. People feel that something is changing; they are now living in a new era, new ideas, and new methods that will bring a greater momentum.

The students at the Normal School for Young Ladies have made presents with flags of Panama and Ecuador. This possibility of an ideal society in abundance creates moments of triumphant exaltation.

The liberals follow the event step by step. The crowd, in groups, raises flags of the Liberal Revolution. Gradually the human masses go down the hills to join the demonstrations. A river of people situates themselves in high places to better observe don Eloy and the railways. In the eyes of the people, it is a miracle.

"Long live the Black Marvel"

"Long live!"

From that moment on, even for the people of high society, it is clear that everyone will benefit from the construction of the train. Thousands of eyes look closer at that wonder, that serpent of strange beauty. The inhabitants of the sierra, characteristically quiet, on this occasion feel invaded by a strange euphoria. They no longer try to hide their admiration, nor can they curb their enthusiasm.

"Long live Alfaro, dammit! Long may he live."

Those present surround the Old Warrior, and the crowd is on both sides cheering him. The Jamaicans who profess their affection and admiration wish to greet him, but the crowd prevents it.

Many people look with amazement at those different men—so robust, so tall, and black—in whatever region they are from. They observe them with mistrust. The dark color of their skin is in the forefront.

Between this vast joy of cries and flags, Leona Cuebute—who is wearing a floral skirt and blue blouse, bracelets, necklaces, and long earrings—waves a red flag. Among the crowd is Marieta Arroyo. She is accompanied by a group of mothers who are carrying a banner that reads: "Thank you, don Eloy." At times, it seems like a miracle to them what Alfaro has done; at times, they believe that he did the impossible.

Marieta makes her way to where Leona is, and they hug each other. Tears wet their faces. Happiness multiplies the joy as they relive their dreams. The Jamaican woman recalls, like a burst of colors made in a painting, that one night, in which anguish burns like a live ember, she went in search of don Eloy, whom she first met at the camp when she was working on the construction of the railway line. She told him that she was spending a lot of time arguing for the custody of her son Rigoberto without anyone listening to her plea; no authority pitied her suffering. Ventura, the child's father, snatched him and did not want to return him. Ventura Villavicencio, a landowner who enjoyed a good income, imposed a series of obstacles so that she could not take charge of her son.

Mired in her despair, she perseveres in her struggle; she dreams that her son Rigoberto were like Alfaro, and why wouldn't she? She cries from tenderness and courage. To have her son in her arms is her greatest desire. With Ventura, he would be no more than a farmhand, the same fate as the other sons of maids whom he had raped, like her. With the sensation of falling into an abyss, she goes to don Eloy.

Such is her concern and anxiety that he is believed capable of any action. Villavicencio (fat, short, and with short legs), who used to spit out tobacco, chooses the maids with an appetite. He joyfully sniffs their fragrance, and his white hands leave macabre wounds on their soul. And after the torture, they felt the fang of another horror; the wives of the homeowners subjected their maids to the greatest humiliation, and they looked at them like leftovers on a plate—vulgar, unworthy scraps. And they pushed them to prostitution.

Leona, decidedly, does not understand what Ventura is saying because there can be no custom or law so unjust. It is impossible to resign herself to losing her son, and now she is embarking on a campaign, together with other mothers who were facing the same situation, who were so horrified that they hide their faces with their hands, refusing to accept the evidence. Disadvantaged and inconsolable, they cry to express the sadness and anguish that sometimes reaches its climax in suicide.

In one of the churches of the city, Leona met Marieta Arroyo when the latter, with deep emotions, was singing prayers to the Virgin Mary, Blessed Mother so that she would do the miracle of getting custody of her daughter Fernanda.

Marieta had been very beautiful. The waves of her black hair reached down to her waist and served as misty framework to the gentle curve of her face. Because of physical abuse, she had separated from her husband; and he forced her to give him her only daughter as a means of exerting pressure on her to not abandon him. Marieta lifted her voice in the firm belief that she would get custody of her daughter. With the religious hymns, she enters an ecstasy until she faints. Living in perpetual fear, in a constant agony, she can hear the voice of her daughter calling her at night.

Tired and crestfallen, she walked limping from the blows by her husband. She wandered the streets singing with a hoarse guttural voice that seemed to be coming out of the pharynx without passing through the mouth. She began to say strange things. Words always related to her Fernanda until Leona included her in her campaign.

With or without the law, Marieta will not leave her daughter in Ventura's possession; and she is seen organizing mothers who have lost custody of their children, mothers who lost faith because of the fear that surrounds them and who worship nothingness, in a return at the failure of being without a pedestal; however, they do not forget their offspring, and they chat in a low voice numbed with pain. At times, they regain their breath in the hope that their children's father sympathizes with their suffering; and they continue to hope that some government official would give them justice.

Men and women compete in their overflow of enthusiasm, looking for new, better, and louder words of praise. Everyone wants to embrace don Eloy and to shake his hands. He trembles with excitement when he hears the rumor and the noise of the people; it is the people who are excited about the huge work!

He continues subtly, severely and discreetly. He demonstrates his ability to control since the affection that the rebellions have for him has multiplied, and his power to govern has increased. The railway is a miraculous fact. He has introduced new energies to the country, to his supporters, and to himself. The benefits have been clearly found, and the economic efforts made are fully justified.

"Long live Alfaro! Long live the Ecuadorian woman! Thank you! We give you the women! Long live la Alfarada!"

"This man has a big and noble heart. Because of him, I have custody of my Rigoberto," said Leona, and she recalls that she spent weeks walking along the sidewalk of the house where don Eloy lived and endlessly waving a small red flag. In the beginning, the inhabitants of the house did not pay attention to her; then one night, a woman's screams, full of anguish, made Alfaro send Lamboreo to ask her what she wanted.

The woman's face was hidden between her hands. She felt despair. When the man asked about what happened to her, she couldn't answer because the words were stuck in her throat; and Leona was unable to recognize her friend Lamboreo. He returned without knowing what happened to her.

One day, Leona woke up early to attend mass at five in the morning; and then after reading, she saw the profound sadness on the faces of the women. She realized that they had the same problem; then, with unprecedented audacity, with a quivering and toneless voice, she spoke to them about the need to organize in order to ask don Eloy to pass the custody of the children to their mothers. All looked at her, surprised and incredulous; however they spread the word to other mothers, and the group grew larger. They say that in any case, although Leona is a black woman, they have to follow in her endeavor because she is linked to the rebellions; and the idea of rescuing their children makes them forget their differences. The project sprouts in the heart of the ladies that strongly beats in them with a force as in a dream, on the very edge of an abyss, as one hangs from a branch to be saved. This removes the last embers of pride that they may have left.

Not all come to the meeting to talk with Alfaro, the head of the Liberal Party. Some are suspicious because their families belong to the Conservative Party, and they delegate Leona to speak with the president.

Among those entering and leaving the home of don Eloy is a young, tall, and burly black man. Leona thinks that he can get the appointment. It takes several weeks; and she bears the evening winds with resignation, but don Eloy does not appear. Sometimes she waits until the last fogs of the city disappear, but she cannot get the interview.

One night, after walking along the sidewalk, she distinguishes the silhouette of don Eloy, who is walking with his arms crossed behind his back. Quickly she runs toward him, but she cannot speak because crying prevents her from saying word. The chief calls Lamboreo to bring a glass of water. The man, when looking at her, recognizes his friend and exclaims, "Leona, Leona!"

She lifts her face and sees Lamboreo. They hug each other.

Don Eloy, fixes his gaze on Leona and says to her, "Girl, you used to work on the rail line. I met you in . . . I believe it was in Bucay . . ."

"Yes, Mr. President."

The Jamaican hastily drinks the water. Don Eloy, with carefully chosen words, asks her what the problem, that torments her so much, is. She says, "Ventura Villavicencio. Ah, how hard it is to tell you everything about my rape! How Ventura abused me! How annoying it is to keep silent about all the details." She must hurry because time passes, and it only just adds to her confusion; and she is aware that Ventura will be leaving the country, taking their child with him to be left with a family member who lives abroad.

Because of her nervousness, Leona cannot express herself clearly. Don Eloy understands the mother's anguish.

"It is my son, Mr. President. He took him from me. I want to have him with me."

"That is why it is called parental authority, beloved daughter," he said with affection.

"We are many mothers who are demanding justice."

"We will provide justice for all."

And touching her head, he says goodbye. He offers a different order of things, of expressions. For the Old Warrior, love is the square root of those who live it; and only love can remove from the human being his maximum creative potential. The maximum creations of mankind have been, are, and will continue to be inspired by love.

Since then, Leona has lived in the house of the Alfaro Paredes family.

A choir of boys and girls is heard; then, the girls of the school dance with short steps and jump to the rhythm of a *sanjuanito*.[16] Don Eloy always gives preference to the youth and applauds enthusiastically. The town's band sounds their instruments and dancing becomes widespread. All pay homage to the first railroad of the country.

Marieta and Leona's eyes are filled with love for Alfaro. They move toward the center of the crowd. Marieta tells him about her dreams. She has achieved victory. She feels like a flower of paradise, and she is working in the post office.

In the city markets is distributed bread with cream, *horchata*, *chicha* corn, potato cakes, *mishqui* gut, *choclos* with cheese, fried fish. It is what is termed "the call of the people," and it is the occasion of celebrating the most important event of the country and Taita Alfaro. Everyone wants to see and touch "the Black Marvel." Now they just think about the railway. They shout for joy on feeling that hope has become a reality, the most difficult railway of the world.

The builders spent months dialoging, in the library of don Eloy's house or in his office, where the most important affairs of the country were dispatched. During the day, they made diagrams, drawings, and lace so that Alfaro could visualize the project of the railway line. And in the evenings, they discussed the project. In this way, it progresses with genuine anguish. The train was covered with the smiles of the indigenous, the blacks, *the cholos*. And the Trans-Andean Railway fell in love with the clouds.

From don Eloy's library came the voices of his Anitilla—his Anita, his Panamanian, his wife—and those of their children, who walked through the corridors. Don Eloy listens very attentively to the constructors in order to later issue his opinion as he did not want to continue without knowing very well the journey that the track would

---

[16] The *sanjuanito* is considered to be the national rhythm of Ecuador. It is Pre-Colombian in origin. It is believed to express a communal message of unity, felling, identity, and relationship with Mother Earth.

follow. He was limited to sipping Manabi coffee—which, according to him, was the best in the world.

So hour after hour, he was engaged in a dialog with the Harman brothers (Archer and John), Henry Davis, and Engineer Wio Benett, those persons who claimed that it would be the most difficult railway in the world. Because the legend said that the devil, upon seeing that the sea had the harmonious musicality of the gods, had tried to put his image on the mountaintop and carved his nose on it so that they would remember him and not travel along these places. Alfaro laughed at such a story, and his eyes sparkled. It is better not tempt the devil.

"Mr. President, the railroad will not pass through the *Nariz del diablo* as it has a gradient of five to six percent. It would be a real danger."

"And then, where will it pass?" asked Alfaro.

"The line that we have drawn is a gradient of three percent," said Henry Davis.

Conservative politicians claimed that the railroad would not be built, that any mobilization of earth and of people would not be suitable for anything nor would it declare anything good for the train. But Alfaro was one of those who quickly recovered his temper, and with more encouragement, he continued in his ideal. There were times when he remained silent, devoid of any commentary, limiting himself to talking with Anita Paredes Bustamante (his wife) and in the company of their children—Olmedo, Esmeralda, Colombia, América, and Colón—who, patient and proud, paid attention to him. They knew it was the most important issue for their father. He told them about the bridges and viaducts that they should build along the railway line; he had become an expert. Concerned about the lack of money, he was thoughtful; then, he smiled remembering the song that he sang to his children when they were little. It was a melody learned at school.

This man, short and thin, loved telling them stories about the weavers of *toquilla* straw hats; and his children liked to hear him. But often Alfaro could not enjoy family life because of the great number of visits he received; however, he sought to get time to reserve an hour after lunch to play with his children. He sat in a wicker chair, and while he entertained them, feigning tranquility, he pretended indifference to the growing problems; and he continued narrating some episode of his childhood although the children understood that he was thinking about other things.

Anitilla gives him a cup of lemon balm tea sweetened with honey, which Alfaro drinks in short sips. Numerous emotions, in an invisible manner, cross over him: the construction of the railway, the exemption from taxes paid by the indigenous, the agrarian reform, the passage of the Church's property to the State, the emancipation of women (which would help to advance the progress of democracy in the country). In order to realize the radical transformations, the Catholic Church has been his worst obstacle, loaded with feudal prejudices. He understands that the greatest risk that he assumes is to remove property from the Church; it could even cost him his life.

Now, everyone wants to record the image of Alfaro and the railroad in their memory. Each and every one of the attendees confesses to being liberal.

The events respond, by *force majeure*, to something more complex and noble that Alfaro awakens. It is the change of the system, his offer to the country to discover new horizons. It is a miraculous infatuation that the lower social strata have been longing for.

The entire city smells of jasmine. Police on horseback, designed to keep order, do the job with great difficulty. From the neighboring houses, whose balconies have been adorned with flower pots in which bloom red geraniums, they throw petals and wave flags of the Liberal Party.

The *guarichas*, who have served the revolution, distribute glasses filled with lemonade; and at the same time, they raise the tone of their voices. They have the feeling that this is the first and the last time that the entire liberal leadership will be united, covered with the revolutionary faith instilled by Alfaro. The *guarichas* have made a promise of fidelity to the Old Warrior. "With Alfaro until death!"

The Jamaicans, filled with joy, are encouraged to join the enthusiasm of the *Alfarada* and the victory of liberalism. They—who are from Kinston, Mendeville, and other regions of Jamaica—after facing so many dangers, have been familiar with dynamite, gnats, mosquitoes, the abysses, snowfall, and the heat. They arrived for the construction of the railway, the link between the coast and the sierra.

The laborers lift their head. They observe the splendors of the inauguration, the greeting that the Ecuadorian people give to the great "Black Marvel." To them, which took years of work and for whom the duty was a constant responsibility. Now they only have left a voice to shout "Long live the railroad!"

The workers' sacrifice has not yet ended. Baffled, they have retired to live in poverty encouraged with Alfaro, hopeful of some recognition, thus, to survive mutilated is an act of heroism.

What happens to the laborers is inconsequential, but no one seems to remember them. Those present only have eyes for don Eloy and for the railway. *Why do not they remember those who sacrificed themselves in the construction of the railroad? They are profoundly grateful to the technical staff, to Mr. Harman, and to others but why not to the laborers?* They are not holding a grudge since the Trans-Andean Railroad is a reality for which they have fought, and they predict the best thing for the train: that it will operate without dangers and that nobody attempts anything against the project manager.

Never was seen a more lively and bustling crowd, with broad-winged *toquilla* straw hats and red headbands, handkerchief on the neck (called a rooster tail), and white trousers. Meanwhile, the *guarichas* shine in multicolored skirts. Never had such a motley crowd gathered. On the balconies, the plazas, the streets, and the markets, they wave the flag of Ecuador along with the red flag, a symbol of the liberal party. From the sidewalks, families shout in favor of don Eloy; but not a single priest is seen. They are confined to their monasteries. For the Church, the railway is its worst enemy as it will serve to spread the liberal doctrine.

The soldiers that make up the rebellion squeeze the spectators' hands. Their leader has reached the end of his long journey that he dreamed about every night. Between criticism and ironies, the project has ended and was completed as desired by the people. They are now in front of the railway, which glitters with the rays of the sun and the beauty of the time. People, steeped in a kind of contemplation or ecstasy, observe the light shining like the color of the homeland, splendid like the light of Latin America as a whole.

They feel immense joy because they belong to the Liberal Party. So much life ahead, so many hopes, that accumulation of desires. They have so many projects! They are surprised to find that the most difficult train in the world would have ended that way. They look to don Eloy, and the undisputed love toward him extends and deepens.

"Long live the railroad!"

"Long live Alfaro!"

"Long live Alfaro, dammit!"

ABOUT THE AUTHORS

Dr. Ingrid Watson-Miller, a native of Washington, D. C., is Director of the Examination for Writing Competency and an Associate Professor of Spanish at Norfolk State University. A graduate of North Carolina Central, Howard and Catholic Universities, she received her doctorate from the University of Maryland, Baltimore County in Language, Literacy and Culture (LLC), and is the first to graduate in Spanish in the LLC program.

Dr. Watson-Miller has researched and presented several papers in Afro-Hispanic literature and culture. She also published a book, *Afro-Hispanic Literature: An Anthology of Writers of African Ancestry* (1991), and published various articles on Afro-Hispanic literature and culture in various journals, including *Afro-Hispanic Review* and *Revista Diaspora*.

She is married to George E. Miller, III and they have two sons, Sean and Simeon (and Arleesa), and three granddaughters.

Dr. Margaret Lindsay Morris is a native of Norfolk, Virginia and is a graduate of Norfolk State University. She made history at the University of Illinois Champaign-Urbana on January 15, 1979. On that date, she became the first Black to receive a Ph.D. in Spanish Literature from that institution.

For over thirty years, she has dedicated herself to teaching all levels of Spanish to students at Historically Black Colleges and Universities in Virginia, North Carolina and South Carolina. Her area of interest is Afro-Hispanic Literature written by and about women.

She is the author of two books: *An Introduction to Selected Afro-Latino Writers (2003) and Discord in the Queen City: The Relationship between Blacks and Hispanics in Charlotte, North Carolina (2005)*. She has researched and presented several papers in Afro-Hispanic literature and culture. Presently, she is the Coordinator of Modern Languages and an Associate Professor at South Carolina State University.

CPSIA information can be obtained at www.ICGtesting.com
Printed in the USA
BVOW08s2149200616

452805BV00001B/16/P